Praise for
New York Times and USA Today Bestselling Author

Diane Capri

"Full of thrills and tension, but smart and human, too."
Lee Child, #1 World Wide Bestselling Author of Jack Reacher Thrillers

"[A] welcome surprise….[W]orks from the first page to 'The End'."
Larry King

"Swift pacing and ongoing suspense are always present…[L]ikable protagonist who uses her political connections for a good cause…Readers should eagerly anticipate the next [book]."
Top Pick, Romantic Times

"…offers tense legal drama with courtroom overtones, twisty plot, and loads of Florida atmosphere. Recommended."
Library Journal

"[A] fast-paced legal thriller…energetic prose…an appealing heroine…clever and capable supporting cast…[that will] keep readers waiting for the next [book]."
Publishers Weekly

"Expertise shines on every page."
Margaret Maron, Edgar, Anthony, Agatha and Macavity Award Winning MWA Past President

ROOM WITH A
CLUE

by DIANE CAPRI

Published by: AugustBooks
http://www.AugustBooks.com

ISBN: 978-1-942633-29-7

Original cover design by: Dar Albert
Digital formatting by: Author E.M.S.
Interior cat silhouettes used under CC0 license from openclipart.org.

Room with a Clue is a work of fiction. Names, characters, places, and incidents either are the product of the author's imagination or are used fictitiously, and any resemblance to actual persons, living or dead, business establishments, events, or locales is entirely coincidental.

Published in the United States of America.

Visit the author website:
http://www.DianeCapri.com

ALSO BY DIANE CAPRI

The Park Hotel Mysteries Series
Reservation with Death
Early Check Out
Room with a Clue
Late Arrival

The Hunt for Justice Series
Due Justice
Twisted Justice
Secret Justice
Wasted Justice
Raw Justice
Mistaken Justice (*novella*)
Cold Justice (*novella*)
False Justice (*novella*)
Fair Justice (*novella*)
True Justice (*novella*)
Night Justice

The Heir Hunter Series
Blood Trails
Trace Evidence

Jordan Fox Mysteries Series
False Truth
(An 11-book continuity series)

The Hunt for Jack Reacher Series:
(in publication order with Lee Child source books in parentheses)

Don't Know Jack (The Killing Floor)

Jack in a Box (*novella*)

Jack and Kill (*novella*)

Get Back Jack (Bad Luck & Trouble)

Jack in the Green (*novella*)

Jack and Joe (The Enemy)

Deep Cover Jack (Persuader)

Jack the Reaper (The Hard Way)

Black Jack (Running Blind/The Visitor)

Ten Two Jack (The Midnight Line)

Jack of Spades (Past Tense)

The Jess Kimball Thrillers Series

Fatal Enemy (*novella*)

Fatal Distraction

Fatal Demand

Fatal Error

Fatal Fall

Fatal Edge (*novella*)

Fatal Game

Fatal Bond

Fatal Past (*novella*)

Fatal Dawn

ROOM WITH A
CLUE

CHAPTER ONE

Dear Miss Charlotte,

I was very pleased to have received your last letter and elated to hear that you are doing well, despite your arthritis, and that the nieces and nephews aren't driving you too crazy. I'm sure you have no problem keeping them in line. You kept me in line for many years.

As you guessed, I haven't been staying out of trouble. I honestly can't believe you heard about Mrs. Walker's death way down there in Texas—and the subsequent investigation and arrest. I suspect you're keeping tabs on me. But believe me, I'm not out looking for trouble. I just happen to stumble onto it. Frequently.

As for your questions about Daniel, I'm going to keep mum for now. I'm not too sure how I feel about him. He's definitely a catch, as you would say, but I'm just taking it slow. I don't want to get hurt again. I don't want to jump in with both feet. That didn't work out for me last time. And no, there really isn't anything going on between me and the sheriff. I don't know where you would ever get that idea. He doesn't even like me. Not even a little bit.

Yes, I've been talking to Mom and Dad. They're always busy, and the time difference makes communicating with them a challenge, but we've managed to talk a couple of times. They still want me to come to Hong Kong. Apparently, they feel since I'm working in a hotel anyway, I might as well be helping out in the family business. I know you think I should go to Hong Kong, too. Family comes first, as you always say, so it's a tough choice. But I love Ginny's family, too, and my job here, and everything about living on Frontenac Island. Which is exactly what I've told them, too. Maybe someday I'll move to Hong Kong—though, of course I'd go if they really needed me to be there.

Frontenac Island life is still great. I will never get tired of the view and the people. The job is…well, it's still a work in progress. I'm still not sure if Samuel Park is going to keep me on. Asking him for a straight answer is like pulling teeth from a tiger. But, you know me, I won't give up until I get the answer I want to hear.

So, that's it for now. I miss you. I hope I can fly down there and see you soon. Or maybe you can fly up here. I know you would love it.

All my love,
Andi

CHAPTER TWO

I READ THE LETTER over once more, slid it into the envelope, and rummaged around in my purse until I found the book of forever stamps with the flowers on them. Miss Charlotte loved flowers. She was quite a gardener. So I pulled the letter out of the envelope again and added a quick post script.

P.S. The Frontenac Island Flower Festival is this week, and I'm really excited about it. The hotel is involved in a lot of the festivities. Some of the events are even held on the hotel grounds. I'll take lots of photos and send them to you if they turn out okay. And I'll even include a picture of Daniel!

I glanced at the clock and realized I was running late. I had a dozen tasks to do for the Flower Festival, and I certainly didn't want to give Samuel any more reasons to be annoyed with me. He found plenty of shortcomings as it was. Time to get moving. I stuffed the letter in the envelope, placed a stamp on it, and dashed out the door of my suite.

Of course, if I'd known this day was going to unfold with me finding another dead body, I'd have stayed in my suite for sure.

The Flower Festival was the biggest event of the year on Frontenac Island. For ten days, the islanders and mainlanders came together to sell products, display wares, and promote their individual businesses or organizations. This was my first festival. Despite all the frenetic preparation and long hours to make it come together smoothly, I was excited to participate. It was the sense of community that I loved, and something I missed about my days at the law firm. We would frequently have events that brought everyone together in a more relaxed atmosphere. From company picnics to big Christmas parties. And Jeremy had ruined that for me, too. Jerk.

As I strolled through the flower gardens of the Park Hotel to get to the pavilion where the tents were set up, I thought about the cryptic message Jeremy Rucker, thieving swine and my old boss, had written on the card accompanying the beautiful bouquet he'd sent to my suite weeks ago.

See you soon.

An innocuous statement, to be sure, but it left me with a sense of discomfort. In fact, I'd been filled with dread ever since receiving the flowers. Why was he sending me flowers? It made no sense. The act itself felt almost threatening in a way, especially because I suspected he'd been calling me on the phone, too. Did he think I had somehow been responsible for his arrest? That I had known about his embezzlement and turned him in?

If that's what he thought, too bad he was wrong. Because if I had known what he was doing, I absolutely would've turned him in. Miss Charlotte would have been horrified otherwise, and so would I.

But the fact was, I hadn't known about his criminal activities. I'd been blindsided by the news, which had resulted in my suspension from the firm while the matter was investigated. Under a cloud of suspicion, I was unable to find another job in California. Thankfully, my good friend and college roommate, Ginny Park, had come to my rescue.

Months later, and I was still in limbo, working as a concierge at the Park Hotel on Frontenac Island in Michigan and hoping to get back to practicing law one day. Even though I was coming to love my new job and all the friends I'd made here, too.

On my way to the festival area, Lois Park, proprietor of the hotel and my boss, cut me off with her arms full of flowers—daffodils to be exact. "Take these."

She shoved them at me. I had to think fast and embrace them before they all ended up on the ground.

"June needs these at her booth."

Before I could ask her for more information, she marched off. Perhaps to grab more flowers.

I made my way to the pavilion, only once nearly bumping into another person and knocking her over, and found where June had been set up. It was one of the showcase booths with a big banner advertising her store—June's Blooms. We expected she'd get a lot of traffic since this was the Flower Festival. Every year, June won the contest for the best floral arrangement. I sure hoped she would win it again. She was one of those people that just brightened up a room. She was also the genius behind all of the amazing bouquets and arrangements at the Park Hotel. If June won, we all won. That's how we looked at it, anyway.

She grinned when she saw me coming, daffodils nearly spilling out of my arms.

"Andi! Thank you for bringing these. I made the last-minute decision to change my arrangement to lilies and daffodils instead of lilies and roses."

I laid the flowers down on her main table. "Why the change?"

She leaned over the table, her red hair getting tangled in the leaves, to whisper secretively into my ear. "Because I heard my competition was using roses, and I didn't want to do the same thing."

"Gotcha."

I glanced over at June's competitor's booth and the woman who owned it. Brittany Gervais of Gervais Flower Boutique. I'd met her a couple months back when I had to deliver a business contract to her on the mainland on behalf of the Park Hotel. She seemed like a nice enough woman, though she paid more attention to my companion, Frontenac City Mayor Daniel Evans, than she did to me. I didn't blame her, though. Daniel was wonderful to look at and flirt with, even if she was a couple of decades too old for him.

The word around the island, though, was that Brittany wasn't really a very nice person. Someone even told me that she'd kicked a puppy once. I figured the gossip was no more than rumors spread by those on the island who wanted June to win the Flower Festival's grand prize again this year. Sour grapes, I hoped, because kicking puppies was definitely not okay with me.

"Hey, June," Brittany called across the pavilion. "Nice daffodils."

June looked over at her with a strained smile plastered on her pale, freckled face.

"Good choice," Brittany said. "Your roses were looking a bit wilted."

"Thank you." June replied with a small wave of her hot-pink-gloved hand. When Brittany turned away to talk to someone who had approached her table, June's smile dropped instantly.

She glanced at me. "I despise that woman." Then she was hustling behind her table, preparing to get things ready to open the booth for customers.

I turned to go and came face-to-face with a killer smile and dimples. My return grin was instant. "Hey there, you."

"Hey, yourself." Daniel was dressed in a lime-green t-shirt, khaki shorts, and sandals. Even in his casualwear, he could've just walked off the pages of a style magazine.

"You're looking pretty relaxed," I said.

"These are my football clothes." I must've given him a confused frown, because he explained, "You don't know about the annual touch football game? We have it every year to kick off the Flower Festival. Islanders against mainlanders."

"Oh, fun."

"I know you're an islander, but you're going to cheer for me, right?"

"Maybe. What's in it for me?" I teased.

His eyebrows shot up. "Dinner later tonight?"

"Sounds good."

CHAPTER THREE

AN HOUR LATER, I was standing on the sidelines with a hundred
other people waiting for the big football match to begin. Each
team had six players. The islander team was composed of people
I knew. Eric Park was the CFO of the Park Hotel and brother of
my best friend Ginny. Lane ran the Park Hotel's front desk and
was a sort of rival for my job. Nancy was a member of the hotel's
top-notch cleaning staff. Then there was Daisy, who owned the
pet hotel and took care of my two cats, Scout and Jem. She loved
them almost as much as I did, for which I was grateful. Karl was
the eccentric leader of the Frontenac Island Historical Society.
Rounding out the team was the sheriff, Luke Jackson.

The only player I knew on the mainlander team was Daniel,
who was the mayor of the town across the straits from Frontenac
Island.

Ginny came up and handed me a drink in a red plastic cup.
She wriggled her eyebrows at me. "Wow, Daniel's looking
mighty fine out there."

I took a sip of the beer and tried not to watch Daniel as he did some stretches on the makeshift football field. Who was I kidding? I totally stared right at him. His head came up, and he smiled and gave me a little wave.

"Lord have mercy," said a woman's voice.

I turned around to see a group of women behind Ginny and me. I recognized a couple of them from businesses in town. They were all looking at something on the other side of the field.

Shannon from Blossom Boutique was fanning her face with her hand. "I could wash my clothes on those abs."

My gaze drifted over and landed firmly on Sheriff Jackson. He'd stripped off his buttoned-up shirt he always wore and was about to put on a red t-shirt, like the shirts the rest of the islander team was wearing. My mouth nearly fell open. The man was built. I had no idea those rippling muscles were under the loose shirts he always wore.

After he pulled on the t-shirt, his gaze met mine. I jolted and spilled beer all over my shoes. When I looked back, there was a smirk on his face. It was slightly cocky, completely male, and kind of made my face flush. Surprised by my reaction, I pulled my attention back to Daniel and the game that had just started.

At first, the match was light and fun. Both teams easily scored touchdowns. Then the second half seemed to get a little more serious. It started when Nancy tackled one of their players—a male who was quite a bit bigger than she was. He didn't seem to appreciate that too much and gave her some trash talk, which was a huge mistake.

Nancy was not one to back down from anything, and she got right up in his face. Both the sheriff and Daniel, since they were the team captains, ran over to break it up. Then the two of them had words.

Ginny elbowed me in the side. "Looks like they're fighting over you."

I made a face. "Don't be stupid."

"Hey, I'm just saying what I see." She grinned.

"I'm going to go get another drink." I left the field and headed back to the pavilion tents and the drink cart.

I shook my head, annoyed that everyone seemed to want to push the sheriff on me. There was absolutely nothing between us but a very shaky friendship. I wasn't even sure if that much was true. It was totally unclear to me whether Sheriff Jackson considered me a friend or not. Since I arrived on the island, we'd definitely seen a lot of each other. In a purely professional context, though. I'd helped him with a few cases, but that was all. He let it be known that he didn't appreciate my help much, either.

As I passed the main pavilion, I heard raised voices. Most of the exhibitors were at the football game, but I imagined there were a few who preferred to finish preparations for their booths. After the game, the booths would get busy.

The flower shops were set out in smaller individual booths. They lined the sides of a large, rectangular main tent. The main tent covered the open fronts of the booths and a large space in the middle where the final judging table would be placed to display the flower arrangements submitted to the competition.

I peered into the far side of the flower tent and saw Brittany Gervais arguing with a man in her booth.

"I told you not to come here," Brittany growled.

"What was I supposed to do? You aren't returning my calls."

"For a reason. We need to keep it cool."

The man grabbed Brittany's arm. "You aren't holding back on me, are you?"

"I wouldn't do that, Tyler." She pulled out of Tyler's grip and stumbled sideways. She had to grab the table nearby to steady herself. Sweat slicked her face.

"You don't look so good, Britt. Are you okay?" Tyler said with real concern.

"I'm fine." She wiped at her shiny face. "Now, leave. I don't want to see you again. Not here, not like this."

"Fine, but you'll regret it if—" He didn't finish his sentence before he marched away.

Brittany sighed and then turned. I ducked out of the way so she didn't see me. I didn't want her to know I'd been eavesdropping. I continued on my way to the drink cart. I spotted June still working at her booth. She didn't look happy, rubbing her pink-gloved hands together nervously.

I reached the cart and collected two cups of beer. I thought I'd drop one off to June. She'd looked like she could use a drink or two to calm her nerves. When I returned to the tent, I didn't see June at her table in her booth. I set the drink down and exited through the back flap of the main tent and walked around to the back of June's booth to look into the area where the cold storage was set up for her flowers.

"June? You back there? I brought you a cold beer."

There was no answer. I looked around and didn't see anyone else in the vicinity. When I went back inside the main tent, my gaze flitted over Brittany's setup. I spotted a pair of hot-pink gardening gloves on her table, probably June's.

I wandered over there and peered into Brittany's booth.

"Hello? June? Brittany?"

Again, there was no answer. I spotted something on the ground. A few crushed daffodils. In fact, it looked like there were several flowers broken and scattered on the ground. From what I'd seen of Brittany Gervais, she was a tidy woman. Obsessively so. This mess was concerning. I walked around the outside perimeter of the main tent. I kept walking until I reached June's cold storage area again.

It was a bit gloomy inside because the overhead light wasn't on. I found the switch on the side and flicked it. The fluorescent blub above flickered to life, casting a yellow glow over everything.

The cooler was unoccupied.

CHAPTER FOUR

I RETURNED TO THE football game with two drinks, since I
hadn't found June.

Ginny glanced at me as I handed her a new cup. "You
missed Daniel's impressive touchdown." She frowned. "What's
wrong?"

"Nothing." I took a sip of beer.

"You look pale."

"I always look pale because I keep out of the sun. Better for
my skin."

She cocked her head. "Are you worried about your
parents?"

I arched my eyebrows. "Why on earth would you guess
that?"

"They're getting older, Andi. You must miss them at least a
little bit." She paused and gnawed her lower lip, which was
what she did when she was upset. "Since Dad died, I'm a lot
more aware of how fragile life is. The way my mom talks to

him all the time worries me, too. Just be careful. Your parents won't live forever. And neither will you."

I shook my head and tried to tease her out of her melancholy. "Believe me, Drew and Emily Steele will be alive to greet the next century. They're healthier than all these horses we have around here."

She didn't say anything else and turned back to the game, but I knew she wasn't buying it.

I took another sip of beer and continued watching the football match. The score was tied, and the mainlanders had the ball. After the snap, the quarterback took a few steps back like he was going to throw, but he handed the ball off to Daniel, who took off like a shot.

As he sprinted past where Ginny and I were standing and cheering, he grinned. I didn't try to stop the smile that spread across my face in return. He ran for the end zone. No way was anyone going to catch him. He had long legs and was quicker than a gazelle.

"Oh, hell," Ginny said with a laugh. I turned to where she was looking and saw Sheriff Jackson sprinting at full speed toward Daniel. "Luke's going to take him down."

As Daniel neared the end zone and the sheriff neared him, I felt conflicted about who to cheer for. The feeling surprised me. I wasn't totally sure my ambivalence was a matter of islander versus mainlander. Which I would never admit to Ginny in a million years.

I could feel the tension in the air while we all waited to see who would triumph. Daniel was two strides away from the end zone, and Sheriff Jackson was one stride away from striking distance.

The crowd gave a collective gasp as the sheriff dove for Daniel, reaching out to snag him around the waist. Then another gasp as Daniel leapt out of the way and landed on his shoulder over the line and in the end zone.

"Touchdown!" someone yelled.

An eruption of cheers sounded across the field as all the mainlanders raised their hands in the air and whooped. A few quiet boos erupted from the sidelines from disgruntled islanders. I clapped along with everyone else.

Ginny punched me lightly in the shoulder. "That was a close one. Our sheriff almost took your man down."

I nodded and laughed along. It had been close. "Things could easily have gone the other way," I replied. And I wasn't sure if I was really talking about the game or something else entirely.

After the football game ended, everyone gathered near the fountain in the garden as Lindsey Hamilton, Frontenac Island mayor, and Daniel, representing Frontenac City, stood on the stage to make a joint announcement and officially start the festival.

Lindsey tapped on the microphone. The high-pitched feedback made everyone flinch. "I guess it's on, then." Laughter spread across the crowd. "Mayor Evans and I are delighted to welcome you all to the fifty-fifth annual Frontenac Island Flower Festival."

We applauded.

"This festival is a time-honored tradition of coming together with our families and neighbors to celebrate what makes Frontenac great. With the help of our friends and partners in Frontenac City," she nodded toward Daniel, who smiled warmly at the crowd, and I noticed a few women swooning, "we bring together everything that makes our communities the absolute best places to live and work and prosper."

Another huge round of applause, and some cheers went up this time, too.

Daniel stepped up to the microphone. "We would like to thank our hosts from the Park Hotel, who have graciously allowed us to use their spectacular grounds once again to host the event." He nodded to Lois and Samuel who stood off to the side of the stage. Lois smiled and returned the nod. Samuel had his arms folded over his chest, and he looked like he'd just eaten a lemon.

I clapped hard. Ginny did a "whoop whoop," which made some people chuckle.

"I would also like to remind everyone to stop by the flower tent today and vote for the best floral arrangements for this year's festival."

"Go, June!" someone yelled from the crowd.

I smiled at that. The islanders were really pumped for June to win again this year.

"So, without further ado or any more talking from me, we formally announce the festival is ON!" Daniel raised his hand and fist-pumped the air.

A lot of applause followed, most of it from the local women. I didn't blame them. It was easy to get excited around Daniel. He had that way about him.

As the crowd dispersed to engage in the festival activities, Daniel came down the three steps from the stage and walked toward me.

"Since it's your first festival, can I show you around?" he asked.

"Sure. I'd love that." I smiled.

Our first stop was at the food carts, which I didn't mind. I was starving. Daniel bought me a corn dog. I devoured it in

three bites and got another, to his amusement. We washed the
corndogs down with freshly squeezed, lavender-infused
lemonade, which was one of the best drinks I'd ever tasted.
Then we moved on to hot fudge sundaes served with incredibly
creamy butter-pecan ice cream all the way from the dairy farm
where it was made in Traverse City. The owners were staying
at the Park, and I'd already thanked them profusely for making
the journey.

After I packed away more food than I'd eaten at one time in
many months, Daniel led me over to the animal pens where he
had to judge the cutest pigmy goat contest.

"Duty calls," he said.

"Have fun."

"I won't be too long. An hour max."

I smiled. "A mayor has to do what he has to do."

He kissed my cheek, then made his way through the crowds
to the judging table.

As I looked into the pen and saw the tiny goats jumping
around and bleating and doing funny things, I realized Daniel
had his work cut out for him. They were all adorable. I spotted
Daisy in the pen, trying not to cry over the cutest tiny goat
wearing a pair of pajamas and munching on the laces of her
boots. Daisy looked up and caught my gaze. I waved at her. I
had a sneaky suspicion she might try to adopt that goat later.

While Daniel performed his mayoral duties, I wandered
over to the game booths, certain there was some game I could
win. I eyed the ball toss into baskets, watching a little girl
bounce them right in and out, which seemed too hard. I moved
on to the dart game, but I didn't like to hear balloons popping,
so I skipped that one. The rubber ducky fishing pond was too
crowded. Which left the ring toss. I paid the guy manning the

station for nine rings while eyeing the giant stuffed unicorn that would look totally out of place in my elegant suite at the hotel.

After throwing three rings, I started to think I'd made a big mistake. Another three rings done, and I knew I'd only wasted my money. Right before I was about to toss the last three, a burly man with a mustache leaned toward me.

"There's a trick to it."

I glanced at him. "Yeah, I've realized that too late, I think."

He chuckled. "It's all in the stance and how you hold the ring."

"Oh yeah?"

He held out his hand for the rings. "What are you looking for?"

I nodded toward the giant rainbow monstrosity. "The unicorn."

He winked at me, settled his stance at the station, and with three quick flicks of his wrist, he landed all three rings onto one of the red-colored bottles.

I clapped, as did a couple of people who'd been watching.

The man turned with flourish and took a bow.

The attendant grabbed the big unicorn and gave it to him. He turned and handed it off to me.

"Thank you…?" I said to the man.

"Ivan." He held out his hand.

I shook it. "Thanks, Ivan. I'm Andi Steele. I'm the concierge at the Park Hotel. Are you staying with us?"

"I am."

"You're here on vacation?"

"Business." He smiled.

"Well, if you need anything during your stay, please come and see me at the concierge desk. I can fix you up with tickets to anything, a great tee time, premium reservations at any restaurant on the island, whatever you want."

"Thank you, Andi. I just may take you up on that." He tipped his head and was on his way.

With my new unicorn clutched to my chest, I wandered back to the animal pen to watch as Daniel put a tiny medal around the neck of the baby goat with the pajamas. Everyone cheered, and the goat bleated. Daniel walked toward me with a grin.

"Nice unicorn," he said.

"Thank you. Her name is Sparkles."

"Where did you win her?"

"Ring toss." I made a face. "But I may have had a little help."

"Should I be jealous?"

I shook my head. "No. Just one of the guests."

"Good." He swung his arm over my shoulders, and we continued our walk together through the festival.

We stopped to cheer at the pie-eating contest. I spotted Wally from the registry office, who had told me he'd been training for this event all year. One of the old-timers from the docks, Reggie, was also up on the podium, tying a red-checkered bib around his neck. I didn't recognize the other three contestants.

"My money's on Tuck." Daniel pointed toward a petite man with Coke-bottle glasses and a bowtie.

"No way he can eat that much. He's too little."

"What do you wager?"

"What did you have in mind?" I asked.

He gave me a look that made me blush. "Dinner and dessert."

Ginny's brother Eric and his wife Nicole sidled up next to us just as I was leaning in for a taste of that dessert.

"Hey, Andi, Daniel," Eric said. "Having fun?"

I nodded. "It's more fun than I thought it would be. I wasn't sure what to expect."

"They didn't have any festivals in California?" Nicole asked.

There was a snide tone in her voice, but I ignored it because she was actually talking to me. Since I arrived on the island, she'd been hostile and standoffish, even after I practically saved her life. Ginny said Nicole worried I'd try to steal Eric away from her. Which was ridiculous. The last thing I wanted was an affair with any married man. The second to last thing was Eric Park.

"I'm sure there were tons of festivals in Cali, but I never had a chance to go to any. The firm kept me too busy." It was true—I'd really never much time for anything didn't involve the law firm. Although the hotel kept me occupied being concierge, too, I'd had time to do some things for myself for a change. Including dating Daniel Evans.

"And now you're busy having fun." Daniel nudged me in the side, just as the pie-eating contest started with a literal bang from the starter's gun.

Fifteen minutes and fifty pies later, most of them eaten by Daniel's ringer, Tuck, we walked over to the main flower tent to check out the flower arrangements and place our votes. There were ten arrangements to view inside the tent, five in the professional category and five in the amateur.

I spotted two elderly women I had nicknamed Blue and Sunglasses—their real names were Nora Gray and Kris Houston—milling about near the amateur flower-arranging table. I'd heard they'd entered this year and were actually plant experts of a sort. All contestants were given two hours to put together a stunning arrangement. Out of the five professionals, either June or Brittany was expected to win.

As we looked over the arrangements, I didn't ask Daniel who he was voting for. It wouldn't have been a fair question. Brittany was from the mainland, and June was our favorite here on the island, so I left him to his secret vote.

June's arrangement was a gorgeous, elegant design. White lilies were shaped into a circle, their stems twisted and braided together, set in a glass bowl, with mosses and lichen and beautiful pink tulips. She must have changed her mind about using daffodils. Regardless, the arrangement would've looked at home on any table in Beverly Hills. I swiveled my head around to ask her about the daffodils, but she was already talking with someone else.

Next to June's was Brittany's arrangement. It overpowered June's in height and color. There were dozens of red roses swooped upwards into a moon shape. Under them was a base of tiny white flowers, and other flowers and fan-type plants curled around the perimeter of the base. It was a pretty composition, but it lacked simplicity and grace. I didn't like it nearly as much as June's.

But some people always thought bigger was better, and there were a lot of folks fluttering around Brittany's arrangement, praising this and that.

All the designers stood behind their creations. When I caught June's gaze, I gave her a big smile and two thumbs-up.

"Your design is gorgeous," I said.

"Thank you, Andi." She glanced worriedly over at Brittany, who was smiling and laughing with a few people.

I leaned in close to her over the table. "It's no contest, in my opinion."

She beamed at that. "I'm so glad you think so."

Then a bark of laughter drew my attention. I looked over to see Brittany lean/stumble over to the right. She grabbed hold of the table the arrangements were on to steady herself instead of landing on the ground in a heap.

June reached for her arm. "Are you okay?"

Brittany pulled away from June and shouted, "I'm fine!" She grabbed the bottle of water on her table and chugged down most of the contents.

As I watched her dribble water down her chin, I thought she almost seemed drunk.

When she was done with the water, she plopped the bottle down on the table with such force the table wobbled. Then it wobbled even more as she tried to stop the table from moving. My belly flipped over when I saw what was going to happen. June must've seen it, too, because she reached to steady Brittany...

Just as Brittany fell over onto the table and knocked her arrangement onto the ground.

The entire pavilion went silent. People open-mouth gaped at the explosion of roses all around the table.

Brittany's eyes bugged out, and she shrieked as her hands pulled at her strawberry-blond hair. Well, more red than blond, actually. Her hair was almost the same shade as June's. Maybe they had the same hair stylist. She turned toward June, nearly foaming at the mouth. "You did this!"

June shook her head and stammered, "No, I...you were—"

"You did it on purpose because you knew I was going to win!"

Daniel rushed over and tried to calm the situation down, but Brittany wasn't having it. She picked up a handful of the roses remaining on the table and threw them at June.

"I could kill you for this! You selfish old witch!"

Then she stomped away.

CHAPTER FIVE

AFTER ABOUT AN HOUR of cleaning, rearranging, and calming people down, the flower tent looked respectable once again and we had all moved on to the next event.

I stood with Nicole, Lane, Megan (the sheriff's daughter), and Carmen (from the hotel's spa) at one opening of the hedge maze, preparing for the relay race. Eric had assured me that if I didn't participate in this particular time-honored tradition, Samuel would be greatly disappointed in me. That was enough motivation for me. I hated that I was sucking up to the old man once again. But I still needed my job.

The other half of our relay team consisted of more Park Hotel folks. Ginny, Eric, Tina (a member of the cleaning crew), Randy (one of the bellhops), and another person I didn't know stood ready to begin at the other entrance to the maze. The object of the race was to run through the maze to the other side, tag the next person, and then they ran back to where you started. Seemed easy enough, but this was a race. Our opponents were also islanders, not mainlanders. There were basically two paths through the maze, and each team used one path.

I was not looking forward to any of this because I had not mastered the maze. I'd attempted it a couple of times—once even at night, which was spooky because I'd thought someone was following me. No one was. It had been nothing but my overactive imagination and a healthy dose of suspicion, since I'd found a dead body in the hotel pool room a few days before and the killer had still been at large at the time.

While we waited for the maze race to begin, I thought about June and what had happened in the tent. After Brittany calmed down—I still thought maybe she'd been drinking or something, because her behavior was so erratic—we'd gotten the table righted and most of her arrangement sorted. The damage actually hadn't been as bad as I'd first thought. The piece had been salvageable, to everyone's relief. Well, everyone except June. She'd actually looked disappointed that we were able to fix things. With Brittany out of the running altogether, the first place prize would've been easily June's to win. Now, the outcome was uncertain once again.

The maze-relay starter's pistol burst like a mini explosion, ringing in my ears and bringing me back to the task at hand. Megan was first, and she was off like a shot. I was third in line after Lane. I worried about holding the team back. I kept telling them that I was a bad bet because I had no idea how to get through the maze, but my teammates assured me the proper turns were marked with little red flags. I just had to follow them, and I'd be through in record time.

Eric came busting out of the maze and tagged Lane, who sprinted into the hedges. Nerves surged over me, and I wasn't sure why. I was usually a pretty confident person. But I knew my strengths and weaknesses. I also knew Samuel and Lois were watching me from the sidelines, and Samuel's eyes were full of judgment. When I glanced at him, I pictured a tiny Casey Cushing perched on Samuel's shoulder, dressed in red and holding a pitchfork, whispering bad things into his ear.

"She'll never be a great concierge, like I am."

"You'd be a fool to keep her on once I return."

"She's not trustworthy."

And the worst one, *"She helped her boss steal all that money from clients."*

I looked away from Samuel, knowing he'd been talking to my former bosses in California. There was no evidence that I did anything wrong, but Jeremy Rucker's embezzlement hung over my head like a dark, foreboding raincloud—despite the fact that I was two thousand miles away and on a beautiful island trying to make a new and totally different life for myself.

"Go, Andi!" I turned to see Daniel waving at me. My smile was instant, completely involuntary. Daniel made me happy. Simple as that. Maybe my new life would work out after all.

Ginny popped out of the hedge and smacked my hand. When I didn't move, she laughed and gave me a little push. "Your turn! Go, Andi!"

Startled into action, I ran into the hedge, cheers in my wake. I took the first right turn based on instinct alone, remembering from the last time I was in the maze. I spotted the red flag on top of the hedge on the corner and kept going. Next left, then right. Then right again? I wasn't sure, and I couldn't see a flag anywhere.

Coming around the corner, I stopped on the path, looked down, and spotted something red and plastic. It was the flag. I picked it up and looked up at the hedge corners; I had no idea where it had fallen from. Great. I was lost again.

I tossed the flag to the ground, then made a decision and went right. After the next left and running into a dead end, I knew I'd made a mistake. I backed up and took the right instead.

As I came around the corner, I spotted a man I didn't recognize going around another corner in front of me. I didn't think he was a member of the other team, and the maze was closed to the public while we ran the race. He had dark hair. A shiver of dread ran down my back. From my brief glance, he looked vaguely familiar.

I followed him into the next turn. I spotted him again just as he went around the hedge. Dark hair, slightly taller than me, solid build, wearing a red shirt and jeans. He reminded me of Jeremy somehow, and that shiver rushed over me again.

I increased my pace and followed him. "Jeremy!"

Just missed him again, making another turn.

"Jeremy!" I said louder as I sprinted to catch up to him.

Right before he dashed around another hedge, he stopped and turned. I nearly smacked right into him.

He wasn't Jeremy.

"What are you doing?" He frowned.

"I'm so sorry. I thought you were someone else."

"You're from the hotel, aren't you?"

I nodded. "Yes, I got lost. Then I saw you and thought you were someone I knew."

He shook his head and rolled his eyes, sweat beaded his forehead. "Well, I'm not." He turned to leave.

"Wait." He stopped with a huff. I asked, "Can you point me in the right direction to get back, please?"

He eyed me for a long moment, then rolled his eyes again with a heavy sigh. "Yeah, go back and turn right, then left, then you should see those flags again."

"Thanks."

He left before I could ask him who he was and why he was here.

I reversed my steps. I turned right, then left, as he'd instructed. But I didn't see any of the red flags. I stopped and shook my head. How big could this maze really be? I must've been going around in circles. I should've brought a flare gun so I could send an "I give up!" signal and someone could rescue me.

Obviously, I was doing something wrong. It couldn't be that hard to get through this maze. I'd survived law school, for Pete's sake. I could do this. I just needed a reset button. Somewhere to start over. The center of the maze. I'd make my way there, then I could plan a path out to the other side. Besides, I was pretty sure there was a map of the maze at the gazebo in the middle.

Straightening my shoulders, I started forward, walking in a straight line, then took my first right, then a left. After another two corners, I was going in the right direction. I made the last turn around the hedge, and I saw the white wooden gazebo ahead.

Relief coursed through me as I hurried over to the domed structure. If I hadn't been anxious to get out of the maze, I would've taken the time to enjoy the respite. There were pretty white wooden benches arranged in a square around the gazebo. On another occasion, I might've taken the time to sit and soak up the peaceful atmosphere. As it was, I was holding up my team. I wanted to get out as fast as I could. I wanted to put my feet up and have a drink. A nice glass of red wine would do the trick.

I stepped into the gazebo to look for the map of the maze. I found it posted on a board inside. As I studied it, a strange feeling floated over me. The hairs on my neck stood on end. I had the sense that I wasn't alone. I glanced to my left and spotted something on the ground outside the gazebo. A pair of balled-up pink gloves. It was a strange thing to see in here, and it made my stomach churn a little. I stepped out of the gazebo and spotted something else near one of the benches. Squinting, I saw that it was a patch of red hair. Which at first didn't make any sense.

Then it dawned on me with dread.

I stumbled down the few steps out of the gazebo and rushed toward the bench. Just behind it, along with that red hair, I spied an outstretched hand.

Oh no, June. Was she hurt?

I came around the bench to see a woman lying on the ground on her side, back to me. A bit of vomit was pooled on the ground nearby. Crouching, I touched her shoulder, and she rolled onto her back, like a puppet no longer on strings.

It wasn't June lying on the ground, mouth slack, eyes open but seeing nothing. A brief surge of relief washed over me, making me lightheaded.

Until I realized the woman was Brittany Gervais. June's competitor in the flower-arranging competition.

I pressed my fingers to her slim neck, to confirm what I already knew. She was dead.

CHAPTER SIX

STANDING, I TOOK A few steps away from the body, careful not to step on anything important, located my cell phone, and called Ginny.

She was laughing when she answered. "Are you lost? I heard you haven't come out yet."

"You need to stop the relay."

"What? Why?"

I sighed. "Is the sheriff there? He needs to come to the gazebo."

There was a long pause. "Andi, please don't tell me—"

"Is he around there?"

"I haven't seen him."

"Okay, I'll call him. You just make sure the relay is stopped and no one comes into the maze." I rubbed at my forehead where a headache was brewing.

"Who is it?" Her voice was quiet, strained.

"Brittany Gervais."

She gasped. "Holy shit."

"Yeah, my sentiments exactly. I thought it was June at first."

"Oh God, Andi. Do you want me to come there? You don't have to deal with this all on your own."

"No, I'm good. Just get the maze closed. Oh, and inform Lois and Samuel, too. But no one else."

After we disconnected, I called the sheriff. He answered on the third ring. "Andi? I'm going to assume this is an emergency."

"Come to the gazebo in the maze. Call the coroner."

"Oh for fu—"

I disconnected before he could let loose a stream of curse words into my ear and slid my phone back into my pocket. I knew I should've gone and sat on one of the benches away from the body. It would've been the smart and respectful thing to do in this situation. And the sheriff would be a lot less annoyed with me. But I couldn't help thinking that I might see something important that others wouldn't notice, as I so often did.

Since I had to wait for the sheriff, and because he wasn't here to stop me, I decided to look over the body and the surrounding area. I knew to be careful not to disturb the crime scene. This way, I wouldn't need to pester him about everything. So, really, Sheriff Jackson should be happy that I was taking the initiative. Although he probably wouldn't view it that way.

I studied Brittany's body first. I saw no obvious signs of trauma. No blood around the body or on it, no bruising or marks on her neck. Maybe she died of a heart attack, or an embolism or aneurysm. An aneurysm could explain her previous erratic behavior at the flower tent, possibly. Not sure it explained the pile of vomit lying next to her now, though.

I got down on my hands and knees and sniffed at her face. There was no definite odor of alcohol, but there was a sickly sweet smell near her open mouth. I imagined most florists carried a sweet scent around them. June did.

Thinking of June, I wondered why her gloves were here near the body. Were they actually June's gloves? If they were, why did Brittany have them? Had she been wearing them for some reason? And why was Brittany in the maze in the first place? I thought it had been off limits to the public for the duration of our relay race, but she'd been here—and that man earlier, too.

When Sheriff Jackson finally arrived at the gazebo, he found me crawling on the ground next to the body. I'd spotted marks on her knees, bits of gravel imbedded in the skin. I figured she must've fallen to her knees first before flopping over to her side.

"What are you doing?"

I glanced up at him. He was still wearing his shorts from the football game, but he had changed into a different t-shirt. His face was a mask of concern—whether it was for me or for the victim, or maybe both, I couldn't tell.

"Just looking," I said as I got to my feet.

He glanced at the body, then at me, shaking his head. "You have got to be the unluckiest woman I have ever met."

"Or maybe I'm just the right person at the right time." I shrugged. "I think about if someone else, like Ginny, had found Brittany. She would've been traumatized for life."

He rubbed at the stubble on his chin. "You should've become a cop. You definitely have the stomach for it."

I perked up at that. It was as close to a compliment as the sheriff had ever given me. "Really?"

Ignoring my eager response, he moved around Brittany's body, scrutinizing it, then pulled out a small notebook from his pocket. "So, tell me the story."

By the time I told the sheriff how I came across the body and what I noticed, Dr. Neumann had arrived along with Deputy Shawn.

Dr. Neumann nodded at me, then snapped on latex gloves and proceeded to examine Brittany's body.

Deputy Shawn sidled up next to me. "You know if you keep finding dead bodies, someone's gonna start thinking you're the one making them dead."

I gave him a hard look. "You know if you keep wearing that uniform, one day someone's gonna charge you with impersonating a cop."

He smirked at that, and I knew he was formulating a retort in that pea brain of his, but before he could say anything else, Sheriff Jackson got in his face. He put out his hand. "Give me the camera, and you go out and canvass the crowd for anyone who came into this maze in the past two hours."

"That's a lot of people to talk to."

"Then you better get your ass going. Now."

After glancing at me, Deputy Shawn reluctantly handed the camera over to the sheriff, then stomped away from the gazebo and disappeared into the maze.

The sheriff fiddled with the camera. "No one thinks you're killing people," he said, without looking at me.

"I know."

"Shawn can be a real jackass."

"I know that, too."

He side-eyed me and offered me a smile, then he was standing over the body, taking pictures, while Dr. Neumann apprised him of what she knew so far.

"Time of death wasn't that long ago. There's little rigor and no real lividity. Maybe two to four hours. I won't have a narrower window until I can take the liver temperature." She stood. "No sign of injury or trauma. So, I can't speculate on the cause of death, either."

"I think she might've been drinking or under the influence of something," I said.

"What makes you say that?" the sheriff asked.

"She was displaying odd and erratic behavior at the flower tent earlier. She was sweating, and she didn't seem stable. She fell over onto the display table."

"Could explain the vomit." Dr. Neumann nodded. "I'll make sure to get bloodwork done to check for drugs or poisons." She stripped off her gloves and shoved them into her pockets. "I'll send in the guys to collect the body."

"Thanks, Doc." The sheriff nodded at her, and she left.

I watched as he continued to take photos of Brittany and the surrounding area. I was surprised he hadn't asked me to leave. Maybe he assumed I was made of stern stuff and could handle it.

I could, most definitely, but I didn't want to. I was getting a bit tired of being strong. Sometimes a girl just needed a breakdown. And a tall glass of red wine. Oh, and an entire tub of mocha-coffee chocolate-chip ice cream all to herself.

When he was done, he came over to me where I sat on one of the benches. He sat beside me. "When one of the other guys gets here, I can walk you out."

I nodded. "Thanks."

"Do you...do you want me to walk you to your suite or something?"

Surprised by the offer, I shook my head. "No, I should probably find Lois and Samuel and let them know what's going on."

"Right." He nodded, then set his hand on my shoulder. "Are you okay? Do you need someone to talk to about it?"

"I'm fine. Nothing a stiff drink, a long bath, and a sleeping pill won't fix."

"It's okay to not be okay, Andi." He squeezed my shoulder. "You've been through a lot of crap in the past few months."

I met his gaze, realizing how incredible his eyes were. Icy blue, but sincere. Some would call them cold, but I found them alluring. "So have you. And you've had to deal with my annoying habit of sticking my nose in things that maybe I have no business being involved with."

His lips curled up into a grin. "You're not *that* annoying."

"No?" I licked my lips. They were suddenly dry.

"No."

It was the most inappropriate time to be feeling something for the sheriff, but it was there anyway. Deep inside my chest, inside my belly. A slow-burning emotion that I was surprised existed at all.

"Andi?"

It was Daniel. He walked with Mayor Hamilton and two other deputies toward the gazebo.

I knew that time couldn't stand still, but as Sheriff Jackson and I gazed at each other, I kind of wished that it could. Just for five minutes. Just to see what would happen.

He dropped his hand and stood to greet the mayors. He dipped his head to each. "Lindsey, Daniel."

"Please tell me this is not another murder." Lindsey tugged at her ear. The lobe was already red. "I can't cancel the festival, Sheriff."

"I don't know what we have yet," he said. "Doesn't appear suspicious, but the doc is going to run some tests and do an autopsy."

"Your deputy is already out there asking people delicate questions."

"I know. I'm sorry, but I want to be prepared, just in case."

Lindsey shook her head. "I'm sorry, Sheriff, but I can't have that. This festival is vital to the island's economy, and a preemptive investigation will ruin us. Please tell your men to stand down—at least, until you know for sure what happened."

He stared at her for a long moment, and I thought he was going to argue with her, but instead he nodded. "Okay. We'll do it your way. For now." He pulled out his cell phone and made a call.

Daniel walked over to the bench and offered his hand to me. I took it, and he pulled me up into his arms and hugged me. Over his shoulder, I saw the sheriff turn away and walk back toward Brittany's body, his phone up to his ear.

"I can't even begin—" Daniel started.

"Yeah, don't even try to understand." I gave a little humorless laugh. "Because I don't."

He let me go and looked over at Brittany's lifeless form. He shook his head. "It doesn't seem real."

"Did you know her well?" I asked.

He shook his head. "Not at all, really. To give her a nod walking down the street maybe. I think the longest conversation I ever had with her was when I went with you to deliver the contract for the festival." He grabbed my hand and squeezed it. "Let's get you out of here."

"Okay."

As we came out of the gazebo, I glanced toward the sheriff. "Is it all right that I leave?"

He nodded. "Yeah, just don't leave town." His lips quirked up a little at the lame joke, then he went back to examining the crime scene and making more phone calls.

Before we walked out into the maze, I thought about something that I didn't tell the sheriff. I'd forgotten to mention the argument that Brittany had with some man named Tyler earlier in the day. From the tone and conversation, I assumed they'd had some kind of relationship. I was about to go back to tell him but figured the information could keep until later.

I needed to get out of the maze and go back to the hotel. I'd had enough of death for one day. Actually, I'd had enough of death for a lifetime. There was only so much a girl could take before it all came crashing down, and I felt I was way too close to that crash.

CHAPTER SEVEN

THE SOUND OF KNOCKING at my door startled me awake the next morning. Groaning, I rolled over to face the bedside clock. It was nine already. This was one of the first sleep-ins I'd had in weeks. It was pretty sad to realize that the only time I got a day off was when I stumbled across a dead body.

The knocking persisted, so I assumed it was Ginny at my door.

"Just use your key!" I shouted, too tired to jump out of bed and open the door.

A few seconds later, I heard the telltale sound of plastic going into the lock, the beep of acceptance, then the slight squeaking of the door opening. Then Ginny came around the corner and jumped on my bed.

I groaned again and pulled the blankets over my head.

"Are you seriously hung over?" she asked, while tugging at my blankets to uncover my face.

"You know I'm not a drinker, and yet you kept pouring wine in my glass."

"I thought you needed it with the day you had." She flopped down beside me on the bed. "I thought for sure I was going to find Daniel in this bed with you. He was really attentive to your needs yesterday." She wriggled her eyebrows.

I grabbed the pillow from under her head and smacked her with it. "We're not there yet."

She laughed. "I like the word 'yet' in there. Gives me hope for your future."

"He was being supportive, which I really appreciated. He's a nice man."

Ginny sighed. "I don't know how you deal with this stuff so calmly. I'd be a wreck if I had found her."

"Believe me, it does bother me. I can just compartmentalize it, I guess." I stretched my arms over my head and yawned. "I feel really bad for June, too."

"Why? I thought she hated Brittany."

"Maybe, but I can't imagine it's going to be a nice way to win Best Floral Arrangement at the festival this year."

Ginny nodded. "Yeah, that would suck." Then she jumped off the bed and pulled on my arm. "Up. We're going to grab some breakfast, and then you're going to come with me to enjoy some festivities for once."

"I need to shower first. And put on some makeup," I said.

"Then get your butt going!" She yanked the covers off me and tossed them on the floor. "We don't have all day."

"Well, actually, we do have all day. Unless you've got a hot date or something." I laughed as I crawled out of bed and headed toward the bathroom. Ginny could always cheer me up. Her optimistic, easygoing nature was something else I cherished about her and always would.

After a nice breakfast of pancakes and fresh fruit and real whipped cream in the restaurant, Ginny and I joined the other festivalgoers out in the gardens of the hotel. Daniel had to return to the mainland, so I wouldn't be seeing him for a few days. I didn't plan to admit it to Ginny, but I was glad. I needed a breather, some time to myself. To think.

The sheriff's unexpected gentleness and offer of support had thrown me for a loop. My head was still spinning. Or maybe it was the five glasses of wine Ginny had encouraged me to drink last night.

We walked through the grounds, pausing to watch a juggler toss fish-shaped bowling pins while riding a unicycle. Then we listened to an eight-year-old fiddler. She had the crowd dancing with her reeling jigs.

I made Ginny stop at the food lane so I could get a bag of hot mini donuts with cinnamon, and then she wanted to do a walk through all the craft booths. She ended up buying four pairs of dangling earrings and a jade bracelet. I bought a candle shaped like a cat and that smelled like cupcakes—I really missed my cats.

I'd been trying to reason with Lois about Scout and Jem, but she wouldn't budge. She insisted that no animals of any kind could live in the hotel. Of course, she bent that rule for VIP guests who wanted to bring their pets. Why couldn't she see that Scout and Jem were my family and living without them was torture?

Next up, Ginny wanted to play one of the games and win a giant unicorn like I had. She was very jealous of that thing. I should probably just give it to her. If she didn't win one herself, then I might do precisely that.

As she tried to toss balls into the wicker baskets, they all bounced out and she said, "I wish some handsome random stranger would come up to me and win me a big old stuffed animal."

She wound up and threw the last one like she was pitching at a Tigers baseball game. The force alone caused the ball to bounce way up and roll about ten feet on the ground before the guy managed to chase it down.

"I didn't say he was handsome," I told her.

The game attendant handed Ginny a tiny pink dog. It looked like a stuffed animal a person could buy in a dollar store for a buck or two.

"But he probably was," she said as she stuffed the little dog into the back pocket of her jeans.

There was something in her tone that gave me pause.

"What's happening with Clinton? I thought you two were dating." We continued our stroll through the grounds.

"We are," she said with a sigh.

"But?"

"I want someone to really WANT me, you know? That all-encompassing desire."

"I'm pretty sure that just happens in the movies."

"I don't know. I've seen the way the sheriff looks at you sometimes."

I gave her a look. "Oh, like how he wants to strangle me when I try to tell him how to do his job?"

"No. The looks he gives you when you don't know he's looking."

I shook my head. "You're definitely seeing things." I stopped at the flower tent and peeked inside. "I want to see how June is doing."

The main tent seemed unusually busy to me. I guess death couldn't keep the flower enthusiasts down, or people were just morbidly curious. What propelled people to slow down and gawk at a motor vehicle accident was the same thing that had them checking out Brittany's last flower arrangement. The pictures they were taking would be discussed for years to come. I could imagine the dialogue. *"Remember when that florist died at the Flower Festival? Well, I was there, and here is a picture of the last flowers she touched. I could feel her spirit in the rose petals."*

A shiver rushed down my spine, and I tried to shake off the sensation even as I craned my neck to get a look at Brittany's booth. It wasn't sectioned off by police tape or anything, although I thought it should've been until they knew for sure how she died. But they'd posted signs warning DO NOT ENTER and placed a few tables blocking access to Brittany's cold storage area where she'd kept her flowers. I imagined that the sheriff had likely gone through her personal things to help identify her next of kin.

If only I could get in there, maybe I could see something the sheriff hadn't, although I had no idea what that would be. It wasn't that Sheriff Jackson was bad at his job. He wasn't. He was a good sheriff, actually. But as a civilian, I wasn't bound by his limitations. Not that I was planning to do anything illegal. I had too much respect for the law.

Ginny caught me wandering in the wrong direction and nudged me back toward June's arrangement on the main table. As we approached, it was like lining up to see the queen. I got a glimpse of the usually even-keeled redhead, and she was beaming and giggling, like she was holding court. After a few elderly women shook June's hand, I was able to push to the front. She startled when she spotted me.

"Hey, June. I just thought I'd stop by and see how you're doing."

"I'm okay. It helps to have something to do. Something else to think about, you know? Thanks for checking on me." Her hands fidgeted with the tie on her bright flower-patterned apron.

"Are you sure? Brittany's death must have been quite a shock."

She flapped a hand at me. "Oh yes, you're right. It is quite a shock. I can't believe it really. Poor Brittany." Her gaze moved away from me and onto the next person at the table.

I frowned. She didn't seem affected at all. I knew people dealt with shock in different ways, but June's almost blasé attitude was a new one for me. She and Brittany were competitors, but I'd believed they were at least friendly with each other on the surface.

"When did you see her last, do you remember?"

She pursed her lips but wouldn't look at me. "I don't know. Probably when she fell on the table and knocked her arrangement over."

"Not after that?"

She frowned. "No." She smiled at another woman standing next to me at the table who was cooing over June's floral arrangement.

"Oh, hey," I said, getting her attention again, "I was wondering…do you have those hot-pink gardening gloves I saw you wearing? I've been looking for a good pair and just wanted to see if those would fit me."

Another hand-flap in my direction. "I haven't seen them. I think I must've lost them somewhere in all this chaos."

"Really? That's interesting, because—"

Ginny pulled me away from the table. "What are you doing?" she hissed.

"What? I'm just talking to June about gardening."

"You were interrogating her about Brittany."

"No, I wasn't." I made an innocent face.

She kept tugging on my arm until we were out of the tent.

"You have no business asking June questions like that. It's rude, if nothing else." She frowned at me. "Besides, Brittany died from a heart attack or something. It's not like she was murdered."

I gave her a noncommittal nod. "Yeah, as far as we know, that's right."

She grabbed my arm and gave me a hard stare. "Right? There was no indication that anything was suspicious."

"Right." I fidgeted a bit and crossed my fingers.

"Andi…" She drew out the second syllable of my name for a really long time. "Why are you suspicious about this?"

I shrugged. "You know me. I can't really let this kind of thing go until I know for sure, one hundred percent."

She rolled her eyes and huffed. "But you don't really think June had anything to do with Brittany's death, do you? I mean, c'mon. It's June. She wouldn't even kill a spider. I once saw her save a tiny little green caterpillar. She picked him up and put him on the grass." She flipped her hair back. "I would've stomped on that little sucker."

I grinned at her dramatics. "I'm not saying June did anything wrong. Just there are some things that are bugging me. Like the fact that the same kind of hot-pink gardening gloves that June has were found near Brittany's body, and June doesn't know where hers are."

"So, maybe both June and Brittany had the same gloves. That's not a crime."

"Why were they there, though? And all balled-up like that?"

Ginny threw up her hands. "What does it matter? It's not your problem to solve. It's a mystery for the sheriff. That's his job." Then she grabbed my face. "Your job today is to have some fun. Do you even remember what that is?"

"I have a slim recollection," I said between fish lips as Ginny's hands squished my cheeks.

"Good." She dropped her hands. "So, now we are going to get ourselves some chocolate-covered cheesecake on a stick. Then we're going over to the main stage, and we're going to enter the karaoke duet contest, and you're going to sing your heart out. After that, if you're lucky, I will let you take a ride on the merry-go-round."

"Is it just horses, or are their other animals to ride?"

"I think it's an assortment of farm animals." She gave me a huge grin, which made my heart not feel so heavy. Ginny was my ray of sunshine and joy. She always had been. I could count on her to cheer me up, no matter what had happened in my life. Bad grades (which only happened once, mind you), bad breakups (again, only happened once), and every time my parents disappointed me (regularly). She was always there with a smile, a hug, and zillions of ways to let off steam and have some fun.

"It sounds like a perfect date." I put my arm through the crook of her elbow.

"Better than dating Daniel?" She wriggled her eyebrows as we set off toward the food carts.

"I have no comment." But my heart was lighter, thinking about Daniel. Not that I'd tell Ginny. She'd hound me even worse if I mentioned it.

CHAPTER EIGHT

AFTER A FUN-FILLED DAY at the festival with Ginny, I was
feeling refreshed and relaxed the next morning at the concierge
desk. Even the tall, spindly woman shouting at me from across
the desk didn't dampen my mood.

"And they wouldn't give us a table." She smacked her bony
hand down on the desk. My little cup of pens rattled from the impact.

"Mrs. Lee, the reservation I made for you was at seven, not
eight."

She curled her lip. "I know that, but we couldn't leave the
card game when Darryl was winning. How stupid would we
have been? There was two hundred dollars at stake."

I wanted to tell her that an unsanctioned big-roller poker
game, which I was positive someone who worked at the hotel
had set up in secret, wasn't a good excuse to miss her dinner
reservation or to complain about losing her table.

"Of course. But you can't expect the restaurant to
accommodate you when you arrive more than an hour late. If

you had called the hotel, or the restaurant, we could've arranged to move your reservation."

"Well, they should have extra tables for emergencies," she pouted.

I tried not to laugh at her. Instead, I just nodded. "Yes, maybe they should." I opened one of my drawers and took out the vouchers for the hotel restaurant. I tore one off and set it on the counter. "I'm sorry this happened. Truly. Here's a breakfast voucher for you and your husband. Please accept my apology for your inconvenience."

She frowned at me, looked at the voucher, and I thought for a moment she was going to argue and ask for something more. But she didn't. She slowly pulled the voucher toward her as if I might snatch it back. "Thank you. This doesn't make up for our missed dinner, but at least it's something."

"I hope you have a wonderful day, Mrs. Lee. If there is anything else I can do for you during your stay at the Park, please don't hesitate to give me a call or come see me here at the desk. I'm on duty until six."

Once she had walked away, I took in a deep, cleansing breath. One problem solved, a million to go. I took out the stack of messages and flipped through them. Calls I needed to make to restaurants to schedule reservations, the golf course for tee times, the ferry to set up two romantic sunset cruises around the island. Never a dull moment working at the Park Hotel, for sure. And we definitely had enough work to support two concierges, as I was going to prove to Samuel so I could keep my job.

As I picked up the phone to make my first call, a man approached. He was a hunky black dude. Muscles, shaved head, brilliant smile, and a tight t-shirt showing off his abs to die for. He had the most unusual, piercing green eyes I'd ever seen, which made me wonder about his ancestry. If I'd been in the market for a date, I'd have snagged him in an instant. Which made me think about Ginny. He was just her type.

"How can I help you, sir?" I asked, giving my standard greeting a lot more feeling than I normally did.

He flashed me a megawatter, and I nearly melted on the spot. "I've checked in today. Here on business. I'm sure the restaurants at the hotel are amazing. But, for variety, can you recommend a few others for me to try?"

"Absolutely." I reached into my desk and pulled out a tri-fold brochure advertising the best restaurants of Frontenac Island and Frontenac City. I opened the brochure and pointed out the one I liked best. "These are all good. But Top of the Lilac is one of my favorites. Steak and seafood, and a farm-to-table menu to die for. Give it a try. You won't be disappointed."

"Thank you." He took the brochure from me, and his fingers touched mine briefly, sending a taser-like shot of electricity through me. And I noticed he wasn't wearing a wedding ring.

Man, this guy was hot! I glanced around frantically for Ginny, but I didn't see her. How could I get her connected with him? It would help if I knew his name.

I extended my hand. "I'm Andi Steele. It's my job to help you with whatever you need while you're our guest, so feel free to call me anytime."

"I'll certainly do that, Ms. Steele. Thank you," he replied and walked away without offering his name.

I watched as he walked to the elevator, but I couldn't see which button he pushed. I considered following him to find out his room number, but then I noticed some of the front staff buzzing about, whispering behind hands, and then running off to another employee to pass on the word. Frowning, I watched as

Lane speed-walked across the floral carpet over to my desk, his eyes flitting everywhere, as if he were about to get caught doing something illegal, immoral, or both.

He leaned over the counter. "Did you hear?"

"Hear what?"

His expression was a mix of horror and excitement. "June Biddle was arrested for Brittany Gervais's murder."

"*What?!*" My exclamation came out louder than I'd expected, and a few people in the lobby swirled around to look at me.

He nodded furiously. "It's true. Shannon over at Blossom saw the sheriff take her into the station."

My heartbeat slowed a couple of clicks, making it possible to breathe normally again, and I frowned at him. "Lane, really. I'm surprised at you, spreading that kind of gossip. Just because the sheriff escorted June to the station doesn't necessarily mean she was arrested. Or that Brittany was murdered, for that matter."

He paused for a second, probably realizing I was right. "Well, maybe. But Shannon said June was in handcuffs." He gave me a satisfied nod, and then he speed-walked back to the front desk.

I couldn't believe Brittany was murdered. Who would want to kill her? She was a florist, for heaven's sake.

But if the sheriff was questioning people, then that meant the autopsy must have uncovered something substantial. I took out my cell phone and dialed Sheriff Jackson. It rang three times and then went to voice mail.

"It's Andi. Call me back right away. There's a lot of talk going on here at the hotel about June."

Just as I was putting my phone away, Lois marched across the lobby toward my desk wearing a heavy scowl, like a storm cloud moving in.

"I know. I heard about June," I said before she could.

She nodded once. "It's ridiculous is what it is. How dare he take that poor woman into the station in handcuffs! Everyone knows June couldn't and wouldn't hurt a fly."

Lois was upset about her friend, but her annoyance was also influenced by June's connection to the Park. June was our florist. Had been for years. And as Lois had told me yesterday when we thought June could win the Flower Festival contest, what happened to June was a reflection on the Park Hotel, too.

"Obviously, something about Brittany's death is suspicious. The sheriff is just trying to cover all the bases, I'm sure."

"You found her body. Was there something out of the ordinary?"

I shook my head. "I'm not a doctor or a coroner, Lois."

"You need to find out what is going on."

"Why me?"

"Because Sheriff Jackson will talk to you. He likes you."

I frowned. "I don't know that he likes me—"

"Oh, he does. I can tell, and I know men. Henry thinks so, too." She fiddled with the pendant around her neck that her husband, Henry, had given her for their anniversary shortly before he died. Lois had been unable to let Henry go. She still talked to him and insisted that he was hanging around the Park, just as he always had.

I wasn't about to comment on Henry's opinions, so I stuck with the Parks who were currently alive. "Lois, I'm a little shocked. Normally, both you and Samuel want me to steer clear of anything that might disparage the hotel."

She arched her eyebrows at me. "This is different. You need to go down to the station right now and help our June. I refuse to believe she's some kind of cold-blooded killer. The sheriff has made a mistake. A big one. And you need to help him see that. Immediately."

I cocked my head. "You know that I'm not a practicing lawyer anymore. I can't be June's lawyer."

She gave me a look. "You're an intelligent woman, Andi. I'm sure you will figure a way around that particular problem. You have done it before when you weren't supposed to get involved in solving a murder."

After another round of arguing with my boss that I also lost, I put the "gone to lunch" sign on the concierge desk and headed out to snag a golf cart and head into the village. The next thing I knew, I stood in the lobby of the sheriff's station trying to sweet-talk Deputy Shawn, who was openly smirking at me.

"The sheriff is busy," he said, then went back to texting on his cell phone.

"I realize that." I clasped my hands to avoid snatching the damn phone out of his hand and tossing it across the room. "Could you let him know I am here, please? It's regarding June Biddle and why she's being questioned."

He didn't bother looking up. "He's busy, and I'm not about to disturb him."

"Fine. I'll wait." I harrumphed, just to let him know I wasn't pleased—in case he hadn't figured that out yet—and then moved to sit in one of the uncomfortable visiting chairs.

He gave me a hard glare and another smirk. "Knock yourself out, lady." Deputy Shawn and I had a mutual disdain for each other. I knew why I didn't like him. He was an insufferable nitwit. But for the life of me, I couldn't figure out why he didn't like me. Unless it was because I was a complete amateur and I showed him up every chance I got. For that, I was not even a little bit sorry.

Two hours and one numb butt later, I heard the door to the back offices open, and June walked into the lobby. I stood and went to her. Her face was pale, and she looked shell-shocked. I grabbed her hand. It was cold and clammy.

"Are you okay?" I asked.

She glanced at me vacantly, but nodded. I led her to the chair I had been using and got her to sit.

"Wait here for me."

She nodded again, and I went back to the counter. "Where's the sheriff?"

Deputy Shawn shrugged.

I'd had enough of his crap. I leaned over the counter. "Sheriff Jackson! Sheriff Jackson, I need to talk to you!"

Deputy Shawn looked at me. "*What is your problem*? I should arrest you for disturbing the peace."

"You, you lazy—"

"For Pete's sake, Andi," the sheriff came around the corner, "why are you yelling in my station?"

"I want to talk to you, and your deputy here refused to let you know I was here."

The sheriff gave Deputy Shawn a disparaging look and then gestured for me to come through to his office. Which I did, tamping down the urge to flip Deputy Shawn the bird as I passed on by. *What a jerk.*

I slid into the visitor's chair by Sheriff Jackson's desk as he took a seat behind it, running a hand through his hair. "I assume you're here because of June."

"Yes. Lois Park sent me. She says Henry's upset, too." Sheriff Jackson cast me an *Oh really?* glance when I mentioned Henry, which I understood perfectly. But he didn't interrupt, so I continued. "What's going on? I thought

Brittany died of a heart attack or an aneurysm or something."

He folded his hands on his desk and leaned forward. "Preliminary tox screen came back. She was poisoned."

I gasped. "Poisoned? Are you sure? What did Dr. Neumann say?"

He shook his head. "You know I can't give you particulars, Andi."

"And you think June poisoned Brittany? Our June? The woman who won't even stomp on caterpillars?" I asked, unsuccessfully attempting to control my incredulity.

He sighed and rubbed his chin. "We have to start somewhere. June had motive and means."

I gave him a deadpan look. "You think June—*June*, for heaven's sake—would murder Brittany over a flower-arranging contest?"

"People have been killed for less."

My mouth fell open. "They have? Really? I'm having trouble believing that, Sheriff."

He leaned back in his chair. "When I worked as a deputy sheriff in Texas, I picked up a domestic call. The boyfriend smashed in his girlfriend's head with an iron skillet because they were out of eggs and he was hungry. So, yeah, I think someone could kill over a silly little contest."

That was the first real personal piece of information he'd ever offered to me. It afforded me a brief glimpse of the reason he'd come to this little island paradise. To get away from the domestics and the murder and mayhem, and maybe the Texas heat, too. Too bad crime happened everywhere, even here.

"What did June say to you? Does she have an alibi?"

"Says she was working at her booth and then went for a short walk through the festival grounds."

"Then someone will have seen her," I said.

"There have been hundreds of people coming and going throughout the festival. We aren't going to be able to talk to everyone." He paused. "Some of those people have already left the island, and we'll never find them. You know how many day tourists we get here every single day?"

I took in a breath to speak, but he put his hand up to stop me.

"No, we can't close the island and sequester everyone."

"I wasn't necessarily going to say that."

"What were you going to say, then?" He cocked an eyebrow.

"Have you talked to someone named Tyler?"

Frowning, he opened up his notebook and flipped through the pages. "Nope, no Tyler on my list. Who is he?"

"I'm not sure, but I saw a man named Tyler arguing with Brittany earlier yesterday, during the football match."

"Boyfriend?"

I nodded. "Ex-boyfriend, I'd guess. Sounded like he'd been calling her and she was avoiding him, and he followed her to the festival to talk to her. Which she didn't like at all. Seemed like the breakup wasn't amicable."

"What did he look like?"

"Tall, about your height, skinny, wavy dark hair."

He wrote all that down in his notebook.

"What was she poisoned with?" I asked.

He leaned back in his chair. "Not sure. It wasn't arsenic or cyanide."

"Easiest thing would be a plant-based poison, considering her profession. A poisonous plant or a concoction of some sort made from plants Brittany already owned."

He nodded. "Most likely."

"Which could also make June most likely." I sighed.

He rubbed at the dark stubble on his chin. "Yeah. Unfortunately."

"Is she under arrest?"

"Not yet. We're still gathering evidence," he said. "And before you ask, we didn't really handcuff her. That's a rumor. Nothing more. So, I'd appreciate it if you'd squelch it when you hear it again."

"Does June need a lawyer?"

He just looked at me, unflinching.

"Please do not tell me that the only lawyer available to her is old man Hobbs."

He opened a desk drawer and pulled out a business card, which he handed to me. "Call her. She's on the mainland but will drop everything and jump on the ferry for the right price. Otherwise, Hobbs it is."

"Thanks." I put the card into my purse and zipped it again.

I had been struggling with those damn pink gloves. But in the end, the truth would come out. If I didn't tell him now, and he found out later that I'd known all along…well, that would not be a good thing. He'd never trust me again, and I wouldn't blame him, really.

I took another breath and forged ahead. "So, you know those pink gardening gloves found by Brittany's body?"

He tilted his head. "What about them?"

"June had an identical pair. I saw her wearing them hours before I found Brittany in the gazebo. During the football game, actually. When I asked her about them later, she said she must've lost them."

The sheriff nodded, and also sighed, then wrote down the information I provided. He liked June as much as the rest of us did, and I could tell all of this was wearing on him. How could it not?

"Everyone at the hotel is very upset about all of this. June is absolutely beloved by all of us." I leaned back in my chair and shook my head. "This really and truly sucks."

"Yeah, it does. But it's what happens when you live in a small town and get to know people." He fiddled with his notebook, opening and closing it. "When you first came here, you didn't know anyone, so it was easy to suspect and question and play crime-solver. You had no stake in the outcome."

I gave him a side-eye. "Is this where you ask me to apologize for being a jerk to you about how you handled that investigation?"

"No, of course not." His lips twitched. "I would never ask you to do that, however warranted it is."

I nodded, my lips slightly twitching as well. I stood to leave. "Oh, just an FYI, your Deputy Shawn is a jackass and not very good at his job."

He nodded. "Yeah, I've come to realize. I'm looking to get him transferred out. But there's not a lot of trained law enforcement professionals clamoring for this beat."

"Well, surely you can do better than him." I walked to the door, put my hand on the knob.

The sheriff said, "But just so you know, I'm not replacing him because he insulted you or has treated you poorly."

I made a face. "Of course not. I would never think you would make personnel changes just because of me." I opened the door and left.

I returned to the lobby. I had planned on driving June home and having a long talk with her to get her side of the story. I needed to know that she didn't have anything to do with

Brittany's death. Because if she had, then Lois had the right to know. Samuel, too. Even though I really didn't want to be the one who delivered the bad news to either of them.

But when I reached the lobby, June's chair was empty and she was gone.

CHAPTER NINE

I SWIRLED AROUND AND glared at Deputy Shawn. "Where did June go?"

He shrugged. "How should I know? I'm not responsible for everyone's comings and goings." Then he went back to his cell phone again.

Instead of launching across the front desk and strangling the worthless twit, I pushed open the main doors and rushed outside. I glanced left and right looking for a curly-haired redhead in distress.

I ran across to June's shop, careful to avoid a speeding tandem bike running down the middle of the street. I pushed on the door, but it was locked, the closed sign still showing. I banged on the glass. "June! It's Andi! June, if you're in there, please let me in."

No answer. I waited a bit, in case she might have been otherwise engaged, before I gave up. I walked down the sidewalk two storefronts away and ducked into Blossom clothing shop.

Shannon was at the window, pretending she hadn't been watching the sheriff's station this whole time. I usually didn't like busybodies, but in this town, it was often helpful when someone like Shannon poked her nose into the sheriff's business.

"Did you see June leave the station?"

Shannon nodded. "Is she okay? I'd be mortified if I'd been arrested."

"She wasn't arrested. The sheriff asked her to come in to answer some questions. That's it. Big difference between those two things." I paused. "I'd appreciate it if you set people straight about that when the topic comes up. It won't help the Park Hotel if everyone thinks our florist was arrested, you know?"

Shannon backed up a step, and I realized that my voice had gotten louder by the syllable. "All right. No need to get upset. I'm as dependent on tourism as every other business on this island is. I know it's not good for one of us to be arrested. And I certainly don't want to hurt the hotel."

"Thanks." I nodded. "Did you see which way June went?"

"She went down Lilac Street, I think. At least that was the direction she walked."

I left the shop, jumped into the hotel golf cart I'd parked at the station, and drove it up Market Street to Lilac and then turned right. I passed Chocolat, my favorite chocolate shop, a couple of other stores, and then I was on Main Street. I parked near the Swan Song bar, got out, and walked down the ferry dock, dodging tourists all the way.

Reggie and JC were sitting at their usual little wooden table playing their usual game of chess. I would swear that every time I came down here, the chess pieces were in the same positions. I suspected they were doing more gossiping than playing chess. Today, as usual, they were in the middle of some off-color argument.

"Bonjour, Andi," JC said, with that twinkle in his eye. I imagined he was quite the charmer when he was younger. He'd probably had a flock of women flapping around him.

"Hey, guys," I said.

Reggie looked down at my hands. "No strudel for your favorite chess champs today?"

"No, sorry. I'm in a bit of a hurry. Have either of you seen June Biddle in the past hour?"

"You mean, Loony Juney?" Reggie twirled a finger near his ear and made a silly face.

"What?"

"Loony Juney," JC said, "that's June's nickname. Or at least it used to be."

I frowned. "Why would people call her that?"

"Probably because of her mad temper. Oh, and when she took gardening shears to that guy's car over on the mainland that time." Reggie winced and made a high-pitched squealing noise. "All the way down the driver's side." He shook his head. "I would not want to get on the wrong side of that woman."

"Me neither," JC agreed with a sharp nod.

"When did that happen?"

"About five years back, I think." Reggie scratched his head. "Maybe longer, maybe shorter. I have a hard time remembering what I had for breakfast most days."

"Oatmeal," JC said. "You always have oatmeal. Every damn day."

"Do either of you know whose car it was?"

Reggie scrunched up his face, making it even more wrinkled than it was. "Boyfriend? Husband?" He shrugged. "One or the other. Had to be. In my experience, a woman doesn't get that angry unless her fella's involved."

"So, do you know where June is now?"

They both shook their heads. "Sorry, but no."

I thanked them and returned to the golf cart. As I drove down Main Street toward the hotel, I kept an eye on the sidewalks, hoping to spot June along the way. I couldn't believe she'd gone AWOL. It didn't seem like her to do that. But as it was turning out, I didn't know June all that well, or maybe not at all. Over the past few weeks, I'd had conversations with her at least once a month when Samuel insisted that I deliver the flower orders for the Park Hotel. We talked about flowers, the weather, and nothing else really. To be honest, now that I thought about it, I didn't know a single important detail about June. How the heck did Lois expect me to help defend her? What's more, did Lois know any of this "Loony Juney" information?

When I returned to the hotel, everyone was running around getting ready for the Flower Festival Ball, which was a fancy way of saying food and dancing out in the garden. It was also when the announcements would be made for the best flower arrangements, so I hoped that June would show up for that. I crossed the lobby quickly before anyone could rope me into helping with the setup. I needed to find Lois.

Ginny intercepted me before I could reach Lois's office. "So, how did it go? Lois said you were going down to the station."

"Brittany was poisoned."

Ginny shook her head. "That's crazy."

"I know."

"And June?"

I gave her a look. "I need to find her. She took off from the station before I could get her version of events."

She gasped. "Oh my God, you think June did it."

"I didn't say that, but the facts are starting to stack up against her." I looked toward the office. "I need to talk to Lois."

"She's down at the tents. The votes are being tallied for the big contest," she said, then chewed on her lip. She did that when she was feeling anxious. "What did the sheriff say?"

"Not much, but he did give me the name of a lawyer. For June." I rummaged in my bag and gave Ginny the card the sheriff had given me.

She took it, looked at the name, and shook her head. "He definitely has a type."

"What does that mean?"

"It means that Paige Weaver is his ex-girlfriend." She handed the card back. "He sure does like lawyers."

I put the card back into my purse and didn't respond.

She narrowed her eyes. "A month ago, you would've told me how stupid I was being talking about you and the sheriff. Actually even earlier at the football game, you didn't want to hear it." She nudged me in the side with her elbow. "What's changed?"

"Nothing." I shook my head and turned to head toward my suite.

"Where are you going?"

"To get ready for the ball. It's formal-ish, isn't it?"

"Yeah."

"Don't you need to change?" I asked with a wry grin.

She looked down at her silky flowing pants, boho blouse, and sandals. "No. This is as formal as I get."

"Okay, but you might want to rethink that approach," I said, with a mischievous smile.

She cocked her head. "Why?"

"There's a real hottie staying at the hotel you might want to impress."

"Why don't you want to impress him yourself?"

"I don't think Daniel's that open minded," I wiggled my eyebrows and grinned.

She punched me playfully on the arm. "So who is he, and how do I find him?"

"That's the first mystery. I don't know his name. But I had the impression he'd checked in recently. You should be able to figure it out by process of elimination if you check the registrations. It'll be worth the effort when you find him. Trust me. Meanwhile, gotta go," I replied, wiggling my fingers in a wave as I went.

CHAPTER TEN

AFTER A SHOWER AND applying makeup and a heavy dose of
hairspray to keep my updo up, I walked down to the gardens. My
dress was a beautiful sky blue, off the shoulder, pleated, tea
length. I'd bought it from Blossom a few weeks ago for this
particular occasion, and it looked amazing. Thankfully, I did not
buy the three-inch pumps Shannon tried to sell to me that were
the same color as the dress. Instead, I preferred to wear a black
pair of kitten heels I already owned. They went with the clutch
purse I also already owned.

I was proud of myself for being frugal. Not having a high-
powered job meant I didn't have a high-powered salary anymore. I
needed to be mindful of what I spent and how I spent it. Especially
since I was also saving up to rent my own place in the village so I
could have my sweet Scout and Jem living with me again.

The pretty fairy lights in the trees and bushes twinkled in the
dwindling light of the day. On top of the small stage, set next to
the stone fountain, a band played light jazz. Music to accompany

the pastries and finger sandwiches people were eating while standing at the tall white tables positioned around the gardens. Some of the guests sat at reserved tables near the stage. I spotted Lois and Samuel making the rounds, chatting with them.

I started on my path to reach Lois and then stalled when I spotted Sheriff Jackson walking toward me. At first I didn't recognize him because he wasn't wearing jeans or his hat. He had on a pressed pair of black pants and a burgundy button-up shirt that seemed to be the perfect color on him. His dark hair was slicked back, but one or two tendrils fell over onto his forehead. He'd also shaved, and his face resembled a smooth granite sculpture. Not that I was memorizing every detail of him as he came nearer.

His gaze traveled from my head to my toes, then back up again. A slow, lazy grin spread across his face, and I put a hand on my belly to stop my stomach from doing somersaults. What was going on with me? I never reacted to men like this. And especially not this particular man, who, most days, made me want to pull my hair out in frustration.

"Hey," he said as he tipped his head.

"Hello." I felt all kinds of nervous, and I didn't know why. It wasn't like a date. Nothing more than two people running into each other unexpectedly.

He turned his gaze toward the other ball guests. "Quite a turnout."

"Yes, although I don't have anything to compare it to since this is my first Flower Festival Ball."

"Right." He nodded. His hand went to the collar of his shirt, and he tugged on it a little, as if it was choking him, which made me smile. He looked like a teen boy at prom, trying to ask a girl to dance. "So, maybe, if the music doesn't suck, we could—"

"Andi!" I twisted around to see Daniel, in a black tux, walking toward us, a big smile on his face. "Hello there." He leaned in and kissed my cheek, then he pulled back and drank me in. "Wow, you look stunning." He glanced at the sheriff. "Doesn't she look amazing, Sheriff?"

"Yes, she does." I met the sheriff's gaze, then he ducked his head and wiped at his mouth. "Have a good night."

"You too, Sheriff." Daniel grabbed my hands as Sheriff Jackson walked off. "Is my unexpected arrival a good surprise or a bad surprise?"

"Good, of course," I said.

He leaned in and kissed me on the lips, nice and gentle. Sweet, even. Then he pulled back and offered me his arm. I slid my hand into the crook of his elbow, and we walked down toward the stage just as Lois and Samuel walked up onto the platform. The music cut off, and the lead guitarist handed Lois the microphone.

"Good evening, everyone," she said. "Welcome to the Flower Festival Ball."

There was a spattering of claps from the crowd.

"Before I announce the winners for the best floral arrangements this year, I'd like to thank Lenny and the Toners for playing our event tonight." The aforementioned Lenny gave Lois a little bow as the crowd offered another round of polite applause.

"Now, for the announcement everyone is waiting for. Our judges have voted. The winner of Best Floral Arrangement— Amateur Class is…" she took out a little card and read it. "Wow, this is a real wild card this year. Nancy White!"

There was wild applause and loud cheers from the hotel's Chamber Crew as Nancy walked up onto the stage to accept her trophy and an envelope with a check for $250. I could hear a couple of faint boos in the crowd and knew immediately it was Blue and Sunglasses getting rowdy for fun. The sisters liked Nancy as well as we all did.

Nancy shook Lois's hand, and they did a grip-and-grin as the photographer from the *Island Gazette* snapped a picture.

"The winner for Best Floral Arrangement—Professional is..." There was a collective intake of breath across the crowd. "June Biddle!"

The crowd cheered loudly, but there were a few comments from some. I imagined these were people from the mainland who were still reeling from Brittany's unexpected death. They might have thought the sympathy vote would tip the scales in her favor. I was a little surprised about that, myself.

I spotted June stumbling through the crowd and climbing the three steps up to the stage. Samuel had to grab her arm to keep her from falling. She walked up to Lois, who shook her hand and gave her the trophy. Lois leaned down toward June's ear, and I imagined she was offering condolences for Brittany and asking if she was okay. But Lois must have suggested June make a speech, because she nodded and accepted the microphone and took a couple of wobbly steps to the edge of the stage.

"I just want to say a few words, if I may," she said, her words slurring a little.

Was she drunk? Had she run off to one of the pubs when she'd left the sheriff's office earlier? I wished I'd thought to look there before I returned to the hotel, but it hadn't occurred to me. I didn't even know June was a drinker.

"I want to say that I'm sorry. I'm sorry that I won this stupid trophy." She dropped it onto the stage. It broke with a loud clang. "As you all know, Brittany is dead."

Gasps and murmurs rolled through the crowd. That's when I spied the sheriff making his way to the stage.

"Brittany is dead. And she should've won this trophy, and I'm sorry. I'm sorry because…" She listed to the side, and I thought for sure she was going to fall to her knees, but she kept her feet. "I'm sorry because I killed her."

CHAPTER ELEVEN

I NEARLY TRIPPED ON the runner along the hardwood floor of
the sheriff's station as I juggled two cups of coffee and a muffin
on my way to the witness room. I pushed open the door with my
elbow and set one cup down on the table near the sofa. I took mine
over to one of the chairs. The second coffee was for June, who
was sagging into the sofa cushions with her eyes closed. Alcohol
fumes wafted off her. The muffin was for me. I was starving.

As I ate the bland muffin, I looked around. It was a
welcoming, comfortable place for witnesses and visitors instead
of a cold, gray interrogation facility. I also liked that the sheriff
let June sober up in here, instead of in a jail cell, before he talked
to her about the confession she made on stage in front of more
than a hundred people. No way any fancy lawyer could ever
argue that her confession had been coerced, for sure.

"June," I said, "drink the coffee I brought you."

She blinked her eyes open, and they rolled back in her head,
but then she slumped forward, reaching for the cup. I picked it

up and put it in her hand. She took a sip and then looked over at me.

"I like your dress. It's pretty, like a bluebell." She drank more coffee. "My head hurts."

"What did you drink?" I asked.

"Wine," she said, then added, "and vodka."

"Did you go to the bar when you left the station earlier?"

"No, I went to a friend's."

"Who?"

"I'd rather not say." She finished the coffee and put her head in her hands. "I might be sick."

I got up, grabbed the trash can, and set it within easy reach. I was completely surprised to see her in this state.

I was getting a crash course in all the things I didn't know about June Biddle. She had a temper and a checkered past, she was a drinker, and she had some secret friend on the island. All of this was a far cry from the shy and sweet repressed woman I'd thought her to be.

After she'd made her drunken confession on stage, she dropped the microphone and pitched forward. Thankfully, the sheriff had been there in time to catch her, so she didn't do a face-plant onto the grass. Daniel and I had raced to the stage to help. June continued to babble on about Brittany, and I told her to stop talking. If she had something to say, she could say it when she was sober.

I'd helped the sheriff put June in his vehicle and then climbed in with her. Daniel had been gracious about the whole thing and promised to text me later. He'd also suggested that since he'd booked a room at the hotel, I could knock on his door when I returned. I felt badly about bailing on him after he'd come to the island for me. Well, technically, I guess it was expected that he'd be at the ball since he was the mayor of Frontenac City. So, it wasn't like he had to make an extra trip to see me. Regardless, I appreciated his discretion in the whole matter.

June's groan drew my attention back to the present.

"Do you need more coffee?" I looked at her as her eyes drooped closed and she held her head in her hands. I felt sorry for her. Making a fool of yourself when you're drunk and then having to deal with the hangover seemed like nothing more than piling on. And that was before we dealt with her legal problems.

She didn't answer me because she fell asleep. It would take more than coffee for her to sober up. She needed a few hours of sleep before she'd be coherent, at the very least.

I walked over to her and, as gently as I could, laid her down onto the sofa. She grabbed my arm before I could walk away.

"I didn't mean to do it, Andi," she mumbled. "She was my friend." Then she passed out, snoring loudly.

I stared down at her for a long moment, trying to decipher the meaning of her words. I refused to believe that June was a cold-blooded killer. Just because she'd said "I killed her," didn't necessarily mean it was murder. Maybe June simply had a guilty conscience about the contest or something. What intrigued me more was the "she was my friend" part of her confession.

I left her there and went in search of Sheriff Jackson.

He met me in the lobby. "She still drunk?"

I nodded. "Yeah, she's going to need a few hours of sleep. Can she sleep in that room? Or do you want to put her in a cell?"

He rubbed at his face. "She's fine where she is."

"Are you going to arrest her?"

"Depends on what she says when she's sober. A confession won't stick if she was under the influence when she made it."

"She's definitely feeling guilty about something," I said, although I still didn't think she poisoned Brittany. Maybe I hadn't known her as well as I'd thought, but surely I hadn't misjudged her that badly. From the way she talked on stage about being sorry, it seemed to me there was more to her rivalry with Brittany. I wondered what it was and whether the answers would help or hurt June.

"Oh, I tracked down Brittany's ex-boyfriend, Tyler." Sheriff Jackson said. "He's coming in tomorrow."

"That's good." I was getting nervous again standing next to the sheriff, which made no sense.

"Did you call the lawyer?" he asked.

I nodded. "She's also coming in tomorrow."

"Good."

"Why didn't you tell me she was your ex-girlfriend?"

His brow furrowed. "Does it matter?"

I quickly shook my head. "I guess that'll be up to June." I cleared my throat. "I'm going back to the hotel. I need to get out of this dress."

He nodded. "Do you need a ride? I could probably get away—"

"Daniel's picking me up."

"Right. Of course he is." Sheriff Jackson kicked at a pebble on the lobby floor and then nodded again. "Have a good night." He turned on his boot heel and started toward the back office.

"Will you call or text me when you question June again?"

"You know you can't be in the room."

"I know that, I just want to be there for her." I paused. "Plus, Lois is really nervous about the potential blowback with all of this. She'll feel better if she hears any news directly from me and before it gets embellished by the gossips.

He nodded. "Yeah, I'll text you."

"Thanks."

I left the station, just as Daniel pulled up in a golf cart from the Park Hotel. I slipped into the passenger side.

"Are you hungry?" he asked during the short drive up the hill to the hotel.

"I am, but I think I have some fruit in my suite." I knew what he was hinting at, but I didn't really feel up to socializing.

"Okay."

He parked the cart at the hotel and walked me to my suite. When we got to the door, I turned to face him. "Thank you. I'm sorry the evening didn't turn out as we planned."

"It's okay. There will be other balls to dance at." He smiled, and I felt my knees go wobbly.

"I hope so," I said in a husky voice.

He walked me back a little so I was pressed against the wall, then leaned in, touching my cheek with his fingers, and covered my mouth with his. The kiss deepened into something a little bit wild and dangerous. When he pulled back to look into my eyes, I was breathless.

"Goodnight, Andi."

"Goodnight," I rasped softly.

He turned to go and then stopped. "Do you want to have breakfast early in the morning before I head back to the mainland?"

I nodded. "Sure."

He gave me another smile and then walked away. I unlocked my door and briefly considered inviting him into my suite. It was tempting. He was tempting. But I had other things on my mind, so I entered my room and locked the door behind me.

First things first. I got changed. As I hung up my pretty dress, I hoped I'd get another chance to wear it soon. I put on my comfortable lounge pants and top, grabbed an apple from the fruit bowl, and flopped down on my sofa.

I pulled my laptop off the coffee table and opened it to do some snooping. I typed *Brittany Gervais Michigan* into the browser's search bar. The first page of results contained a couple of social media accounts and a link to a web page for her company—Gervais Flower Boutique. I clicked on the link and scrolled through the web page. I saw nothing out of the ordinary. Just the usual photos of flower arrangements, pricing, contact info, how to order, and a few testimonials from satisfied customers. Nothing revealing. Certainly nothing that suggested Brittany had enemies who might want to kill her.

Next, I went into her social media accounts. She had a good amount of followers, but the pages consisted of photos of the spectacular flower arrangements she'd created over the last few years. There didn't seem to be any personal photos. I clicked on her followers list to see if June was listed. She was, but that could have been strictly because she wanted to keep an eye on her competitor. It was smart to see what others were doing. Brittany followed June as well. So, they were engaged in mutual snooping, if that's what it was.

On another social media site, fifty different women named Brittany Gervais were listed. I drilled down and, after a few minutes, found Brittany's business page. I scrolled through it, made note of her connections, her past places of employment and where she went to school, which wasn't recently. Brittany and June were about the same age. Both were in their mid-forties. I searched to see if June had an account. There had to be a commonality between these two. Maybe they really were friends, offline as well as on. If so, when had they become friends and when had they fallen out? And why?

Searching through June's pages, I scrolled past her bio, her current and past employment, and stopped on where she went to school. That was the connection. They both attended the same college for a business degree. Okay, so I had a connection, although it was tenuous, and a time range. Perhaps I could find something stronger that linked them. Once I found that, then I might learn what broke their friendship.

My stomach growled, so I ate my apple while I considered the best way forward. In some ways, it was too bad I couldn't actually be June's lawyer. The good news was that I wasn't bound by certain rules, either. Not that I would do anything illegal, because I wouldn't.

Taking a wild chance, I typed *Brittany Gervais and June Biddle Michigan* into the search engine. After flipping through a couple of pages, I found a small article about alumni from the college where they'd both graduated the same year. I kept scrolling and didn't find anything else. On a whim, I clicked on a search for images featuring the two of them.

I went through hundreds of images. I found nothing but kept going. I was determined to find something, if it existed. Then, after scrolling for what seemed like an hour, I spotted a photo from a wedding photographer in Ann Arbor. Underneath, the caption read: *Simon and Brittany Gervais wedding 2008.* I clicked on it, and it sent me to a wedding album on the photographer's site. I clicked on the photo of the bride and groom and enlarged it, squinting at the bride. It was definitely Brittany. So, she was married ten years ago and obviously later divorced, since she was dating this Tyler guy.

I flipped through the photos, bride and groom together in every imaginable combination. Then there were photos of the bride's family and the groom's. Next came the wedding party photos. I flipped through two then stopped. I enlarged the bridal party, focusing on one face in particular. The maid of honor was where my persistence paid off.

Ten years ago, when Brittany married Simon Gervais, June Biddle had been Brittany's maid of honor.

Which meant they had, most definitely, been friends.

CHAPTER TWELVE

I DIDN'T SLEEP WELL, so when I met Daniel for breakfast at the hotel restaurant at eight, I kept yawning and apologizing for yawning.

"I take it you didn't go to sleep right after I dropped you off," he commented as he signaled for our server to pour more coffee.

"No. I ended up online for hours."

"Learn anything interesting?"

I slathered jam over my English muffin. "Yeah, that June Biddle and Brittany Gervais were good friends. They graduated from the same college in the same year. And June was the maid of honor in Brittany's wedding." I took a bite. "I'd love to know when they fell out and why."

"Well, I do know their rivalry for the Flower Fest trophy has been going on for five years now. So I'd guess they must've fallen out before then."

"Did they own their individual shops before then?"

"I don't know." He finished the last of his egg-white omelet and set down the fork.

I gave him a wide, flirty grin.

He shook his head, but his lips curled up. "Yes, I can find out about Brittany's shop for you. You're on your own with June's."

"Thank you. I owe you."

"When I get the info, you can come to Frontenac City to retrieve it, and I'll cook you dinner at my place." There was a bit of a sparkle in his blue eyes that made my heart skip a beat.

"Deal," I said breathlessly.

He set his napkin on the table. "Now I have to go if I want to catch the ferry in time to make my morning meetings." He stood, leaned down, and kissed me before I could get to my feet and hug him. "I'll talk to you later."

Lois took that exact moment to approach the table. "Good morning, Mayor Evans," she said wryly.

"Good morning, Lois. Thanks to you and your staff, the festival was a resounding success once again, despite the tragedy of Ms. Gervais's sudden death."

"Yes, that was a shock, but I think all in all, yes, it was a success."

"I have to run. It was nice to see you." He nodded toward Lois, then winked at me and went striding out of the restaurant.

I was about to stand, to pay the bill and get to work, but Lois sat in Daniel's vacated chair. So I stayed put.

"When did this happen?" she asked, referencing my breakfast with Daniel.

"Couple of months now."

She nodded. "I see."

"Do you disapprove? Is there something about Daniel I should know?"

"No, he's a good guy as far as I know. I just don't see him as your type." Her tone was more judgmental than motherly.

I was about to ask what she thought my type was, but I didn't because I feared she was going to say "handsome, rugged, dogged, loyal, stubborn, and looks amazing in a pair of jeans and cowboy hat." So, I refrained from asking and, instead, finished my English muffin.

"How is June?" she asked.

"Last I saw her, she was sleeping it off on the sheriff's couch." I drank the rest of my coffee, knowing I was going to need the extra caffeine. "He was planning to question her again later this morning."

She played with the sugar packets on the table. "I refuse to believe she had anything to do with that woman's death."

"Did you know that she and Brittany were good friends once upon a time?"

She frowned. "No, I didn't."

"They had a serious falling out if June actually killed her, don't you think?"

"Doesn't mean…" she stammered.

"How long has June had her shop on the island?"

"About six years."

"As far as you know, is her business solvent? She's not having any money troubles?"

Lois made a face. "I assume she's doing well. She gets all our business, and flowers are not cheap."

I nodded just as my cell phone buzzed. I checked it to see a text from the sheriff.

Tyler is here for questioning. Also, I'll be talking to June right after.

"I've got to go. The sheriff is planning to question June." I stood. "Can someone handle my desk for the rest of the morning?"

Lois nodded. "Lane will jump at the chance to do it."

Yeah, I bet he will. It seemed everyone wanted my job. Not only did I have to worry about Casey coming back to work, but now I had the upstart Lane from the front desk clamoring to take my place. I needed to have another talk with Samuel about all of this. I needed some assurances. Having Lois on my side would be a big bonus, but I'd seen her kowtow to him too many times to believe she could or would overrule him if he wanted me fired.

I said, "Hey, I'm doing a good job for you, aren't I?"

"Yes, absolutely." She frowned and eyed me carefully.

"It's just that, with Casey returning soon…"

She put her hand on my shoulder and squeezed. "Don't worry. I have your back. As does Ginny, of course."

"And what about Eric and Nicole?"

"Well, you know how Nicole can be…"

"I saved her life."

She shrugged. "True, but that only goes so far. And did you really save her life? I mean, a serious injury, certainly."

Although I begged to differ, I didn't say anything.

"And Eric basically does just about everything Nicole says," she said.

"What about the staff?" I asked, feeling a little more nervous instead of less.

"Oh, they all love you. Well, maybe not everyone, but mostly all of the staff. Some think you can be a bit bossy. Oh, and a bit nosey…"

I put my hand up in defense. "Okay, I get it. I have some work to do if I'm to become indispensable."

Lois smiled and nodded. "If it's any consolation, dear, Henry loves you. He thinks of you like a daughter. Always has."

I smiled, too and lightly touched her arm. "He was always good to me."

She straightened as if my sympathy bothered her, then she was back to Business Lois. "I take it you're going to the station."

I nodded.

"I have some stuff that needs to be taken down to the village."

"What stuff?"

"Just a few boxes, nothing major."

As I left the hotel, driving a golf cart packed with the "nothing major" boxes which were stacked three high and three wide, I thought about how Lois had talked about her late husband, Henry. In the present tense. She never talked about him in the past tense. It was worrisome.

Ginny told me she and Eric had caught their mom a time or two having conversations with Henry around the hotel, and I had, too. I really hoped Lois's conversations with Henry weren't an indication of mental illness. It made me wonder if Samuel's return to the hotel wasn't necessarily all about me. Perhaps I'd been a convenient excuse. Maybe he was really worried about Lois instead.

When I arrived at the station, carrying one of the boxes inside with me, there were a few people milling about. One older man was talking to Deputy Shawn at the counter, and there was a tired-looking woman sitting in one of the visitor chairs. She actually looked a lot like Brittany in her face and stature, and she had the same fair skin and reddish hair. A relative? I placed Lois's box by the counter, and I sat in a chair near the woman.

I looked over at her, sizing her up. I didn't want to intrude on her grief, but I wanted some answers for June's sake. "Are you here about Brittany Gervais?"

Her head came up. "Yes, she was my sister."

"I'm so sorry for your loss."

"Thank you," she said. "Did you know her?"

I nodded. "Not well, though. We'd only talked a few times. She was a lovely woman."

She frowned. "You couldn't have known her well if you think that."

Oops.

"Do you know June Biddle, then?"

Her face darkened. "Yeah, I know *her*. She ruined Britt's life years ago—over Simon."

"Simon?"

"Yeah, Simon, Britt's ex-husband." She made a face. "Are you sure you even knew her?"

Before I could respond, the door to the back rooms opened, and Tyler walked out, followed by the sheriff, who frowned when he spotted me.

Brittany's sister stood as Tyler approached. "Are you done? Can we leave now? I hate this island."

His gaze skimmed over me, unsure if he knew me or not.

I offered my hand to him. "I'm sorry for your loss. It's Tyler, right?"

Nodding, he took my hand, and I noticed a very angry-looking red rash on the back of his hand that traveled up to his wrist.

Brittany's sister stepped in between us and grabbed his arm. "Let's go."

As she pulled him out of the station, her hand went into his, and they walked out like that, which I found a bit odd, considering the circumstances. Sheriff Jackson came up to me. "What was that all about?"

"Just offering my condolences."

His eyebrows arched up, and he stared at me unblinking.

"Did you notice the rash on his hand?" I asked, hoping he'd stop giving me that disappointed look.

"Yup, it's on both hands," he said.

"Did you ask about it?"

"He said it was eczema."

"You can get a rash like that from certain types of plants."

His eyes narrowed. "What kind of plants?"

"Poisonous ones, I imagine."

He nodded, rubbed at his chin. "Do we know any plant experts?"

I nodded. "Two. One is in the morgue, and the other is in your witness room."

"I'll call Doc Neumann. Maybe she can find us a plant specialist." He frowned again.

"What?"

He shook his head.

"No, it looked like you thought of something."

"Maybe. Could be nothing."

I could tell he'd had some sort of epiphany, and I wanted to know what it was. But he wouldn't simply tell me. I'd have to needle it out of him. And not some tiny pin, either. More like a hypodermic needle big enough for a horse, complete with plunger.

"Are you going to question June now?"

"Yeah, just getting set up."

I glanced down at the box near the counter. "Oh yeah, Lois sent me down with a bunch of boxes of stuff for you."

"What's in the boxes?"

"I don't even know." I crouched to pick up the box I'd brought in. As I bent over, my cell phone slid out of my purse. I set the box down for a second to scramble for my phone on the floor. After much scrambling, I picked it up and slid it into my purse, just as the door to the back offices opened and a blond woman in a gray skirt and white blouse walked out. The heel of her black pump caught on the box I'd set down. She stumbled to the side and grabbed the back of a nearby chair to steady herself so she didn't fall.

"Who the HELL left this box here?!" Her gaze was fierce as she glared around at the room. "I could've broken my neck!"

Slowly, I raised my hand. "Me."

She pinned me with her fiery gaze until I was actually terrified.

Before she could launch a full-fledged attack, Sheriff Jackson stepped between us. "Paige, this is Andi Steele." He glanced at me. "Andi, this is Paige Weaver, the lawyer I told you about."

Paige took a deep breath and then let it out, and her entire composure changed. It was phenomenal to witness. She put on a polite smile and held out her hand. I noticed her manicured nails and felt very self-conscious about mine, which hadn't been professionally manicured since I'd left California.

"Andi, it's very nice to meet you. Thank you for calling me for June."

I shook her hand. "It's good to meet you, too."

She took a moment to look me over and then swept a hand across her perfectly coifed hair. "I have heard a lot about you."

"All good, I hope," I said with a chuckle.

She gave me that shellacked toothy smile. I was positive that she'd put Vaseline on her teeth to make them shine. "Your former colleagues in California speak…fondly of you."

Why the hell would she have called my old firm? Why was she checking up on me?

"Well, you have me at a disadvantage, because I haven't heard a single thing about you." I instinctively stepped closer to the sheriff. "He didn't even tell me you two had dated."

The sheriff's eyebrows shot upward into his hairline. Paige noticed, and her hackles rose. Ah. Mission accomplished. Just as I'd thought. She still had feelings for Sheriff Jackson. I tucked the knowledge away for the moment, certain it would come in handy later.

She smiled at the sheriff. "Shall we get this done? My client needs to get home and get some rest. She's been through an extremely unfortunate, traumatic experience."

"Yeah." He nodded and then looked at me. I swore he was scolding me with that frown. "I'll make sure Shawn gets the boxes out of your cart."

"Great. Thanks."

Paige glanced at me. "Nice to have met you, Andi. Now that I'm here, you're no longer needed."

"You too, Paige," I replied, making the effort to sound professional.

Sheriff Jackson opened the door to the back rooms, and Paige followed him through. Before she stepped over the threshold, she glanced back at me. "I hope you remember that June is *my client*. I'm the one with a license to practice here. This won't be amateur hour." Then she went through the door and let it shut firmly behind her.

Too bad the heavy door didn't smack her in the ass.

CHAPTER THIRTEEN

AMATEUR HOUR. AMATEUR HOUR! I thought with an
indignant sniff.

This mantra repeated in my head on an endless loop. By the
time I got back to the hotel, I must've looked like I was going to
rip someone's throat out, because people avoided me, both staff
and guests. After being stung by Paige's well-aimed barb, I'd
endured twenty minutes of Deputy Shawn's angry efforts to
unload the golf cart.

"So, I guess I have you to thank for the upcoming transfer,"
he'd snapped as he grabbed two boxes from the back.

"I don't know what you are talking about."

"Right. Everything was fine until you showed up on the
island."

"I still don't know what you are talking about," I said,
although I was pretty sure I did know. The sheriff had mentioned
something about transferring Shawn off the island. But it was his
own incompetence that got him booted, not my influence.

"You must have the sheriff wound around your little finger. He'd never have thought of getting rid of me unless you'd said something to him."

I glared at him. "Maybe it's the fact that you are lazy, incompetent, and really, truly suck at your job. Maybe *that's* why the sheriff wants to get you the hell off this island." I took a step toward him, indignant fire raging inside. "You are not cut out to be in law enforcement."

Then I'd grabbed the last box out of the cart and accidentally (deliberately, if I'm honest) dropped it onto his foot. I jumped into the cart and peeled out of the parking lot. I'd actually burned a little rubber, which made me feel a bit better.

Ginny intercepted me as I stormed across the lobby. "You look like you want to kill someone, or have already."

"It was close." I held up my thumb and forefinger, almost touching. "This close."

When Lane saw me approaching the concierge desk, he logged off the computer and came around the other side.

"How did it go?" I asked him, doing my best not to snap his head off. After all, he wasn't responsible for Deputy Shawn's outrageous accusations.

"Lots of people checking out. So, lots of taxi and shuttle arranging, and bag storing."

I figured as much, since the festival had ended with last night's ball. I got behind the desk and stashed my purse in one of the cupboards. "Thanks for covering for me."

He gave me a big smile. "It was no problem. I always enjoy helping out." He returned to the front desk, his usual post.

"You know he said that because you were standing here," I said to Ginny.

"I know. He's the ultimate suck-up. Samuel loves 'im for it."
She shook her head. "Lois said you went down to the station.
Did everything go okay? Is June…?" She shrugged, probably not
sure exactly what to ask. The evidence against June was
mounting, and there was talk around the hotel, and none of it was
good.

"You know her better than I do," I replied.

Ginny worried at her bottom lip. "She's always been a
pleasant person. I've never seen her angry or even in a bad
mood. I don't think she's capable of murder."

"We're all capable in the right set of circumstances," I
growled, thinking of Deputy Shawn's foot again.

Ginny shrugged, and I could almost see her shifting gears as
her mischievous grin returned. "So, I found out his name."

"Who's name?"

"The major hottie you are trying to set me up with. Wasn't
easy to find, either, with all the extra guests for the Flower
Festival coming and going."

"So, are you going to make me guess or what?" I teased.

"I should. That would serve you right." She squeezed my
arm. "*Barrington.* How's that for a name? Sounds positively
regal, doesn't it?"

"That's his first name or his last name?"

"Does it matter? Either way, it sounds impressive. And get
this. He's here all the way from Hong Kong. Wonder if your
parents know anything about him?" Someone called to her from
across the room. She looked over and then turned to go. "Sorry.
We'll pick this up later."

I lost myself in work for the rest of the afternoon and tried
not to think about Barrington, or June, or Shawn, or that horrible
woman, Paige. What had the sheriff ever seen in her? It made me

question his judgment for dating her. Maybe I'd just caught her on a bad day. Yeah, and maybe the devil was missing his mistress.

After I helped a couple book a tee time on the golf course—it was their forty-fifth wedding anniversary and they'd met during a golf tournament. He was golfing and she was a caddy for another golfer—I got a bit of a breather. I checked my phone and saw a text from Daniel asking how my day was going. I texted back with a thumbs-down and cry-face emoji, then I rushed across the lobby to the tea shop.

While I waited for my tea and tried not to think about Barrington from Hong Kong, I looked around the café, taking in the different people sitting at tables. That was one of the things I liked about being concierge—people watching. So many types of men and women have walked through those hotel doors.

My gaze landed on two clean-cut men huddled together at a small table, drinking tea and eating sandwich wraps. They both wore lightweight hoodies and track pants but looked undeniably uncomfortable in them. It was as if they were wearing costumes, a disguise even.

I wondered what they were discussing so seriously, so I took a step toward their table, straining to hear their conversation.

"Last I heard, he left the island," the blond one said.

"Yeah, but we need to find out why he was here and who he's been talking to," the balding one said, then bit into his food.

The blond shook his head. "Tyler is going to be in a lot of trouble when the bigwigs catch up to him."

Baldy nodded in agreement.

Tyler? The same Tyler she'd seen at the sheriff's station? The one who'd been arguing with Brittany and left the station with Brittany's sister? Why were these guys looking for Tyler?

And who were these guys, anyway? They definitely didn't look like mobsters. They didn't look like athletes, either.

I grabbed my tea and decided to welcome them to the hotel and offer my concierge services. "Hello there," I said.

They both startled and glanced up at me.

I gave them my winningest smile. "I'm Andi Steele, the concierge here at the Park. I just wanted to welcome you to the hotel. If there is anything I can do to help make your stay a pleasant experience, simply let me know."

Blondie looked at Baldy, who then glanced wide-eyed at me. "No, thank you. I'm pretty sure we're all set."

"Dinner reservations? Tee time? You two look like golfers."

"Nope, we are definitely not golfers," Baldy said.

"I like to golf," Blondie said.

Baldy frowned. "But that's not why we're here."

"You're here on business or pleasure?" I spied the receipt for their meal on the table wondering if their room number was on it.

Blondie said, "Pleasure." At the same time, Baldy said, "Business."

I had to hold back a laugh. If these two were spying, they weren't very good at it.

"Well, there's always time for both," I said, then I pulled out a card from my pocket and held it out to Baldy, but I dropped it onto the table. "Oh, I'm sorry." I scrambled for it, swiping the receipt. I handed the card to Baldy. "If you change your mind, don't hesitate to call my desk."

"Thank you." He opened his wallet to put my card in, and I spotted an ID card from Ackerman Biosystems along with his Costco membership and a Delta Airlines frequent flyer card.

"Have a good day." I then beelined back to my desk and logged on to the hotel server. I unrumpled the receipt and looked down at the bottom of it. They'd charged their lunch to room 312. I plugged the number into the system.

Room 312 was registered under the name Barry Laughlin. Checked in this morning to a room with two double beds.

I then went on the internet and searched for Ackerman Biosystems. The first entry that showed was from a company in Ann Arbor. I clicked on the link. *Ackerman Biosystems empowers innovators to unlock the global genetic potential of plants.* I scrolled through the pages. Ackerman was a bioengineering company finding ways to optimize crops by capitalizing on genetic diversity. So, they were basically fooling around with plant DNA and making new plants or changing how other plants grow. In other words, GMOs.

In the company's search bar, I typed in Barry Laughlin. A page listing current employees at Ackerman displayed them in alphabetical order. I scrolled down and found a picture of baldy from the café. Trent Mason. He was listed as a chief bioengineer. There was no photo of Blondie—Keith Dubber, but he looked like some sort of engineer to me, too.

What was a bioengineer doing on the island looking for Tyler, who just happened to somehow be involved with a dead florist? It didn't make sense, except that the common denominator was plants.

Brittany and June worked with plants and flowers. Obviously, Tyler did, too, since he was somehow connected to the same company as the two guys in the café. Brittany died from some mysterious poison that I'd bet a million bucks was plant related. And the sheriff said Tyler had a rash on his hands that I suspected was plant related, too. And now these two bio-engineers were here looking for Tyler.

What was going on, and who knew the plant business could be deadly?

Obviously, I had a lot to learn about plants. Especially poisonous ones.

The sheriff had said he planned to contact a plant expert, but I couldn't wait for that to happen. And it wasn't like he would share any information with me, anyway. So I needed to find my own plant expert.

Who did I know with a green thumb who would talk openly to me?

I smiled, realizing I knew two green thumbs who loved to talk.

CHAPTER FOURTEEN

BY THE TIME I parked the hotel cart in front of Nora and Kris's little bungalow, it was late. I was pretty sure the eighty-year-old sisters would still be up. They were both firecrackers and had more energy than some of the younger people I knew.

I knocked on their door. Five seconds later, I could hear one of them shouting, "Someone's at the door!"

Then the response. "So, why don't you get it?"

"I'm in my nightie."

"So am I."

"Well, yours isn't see-through. Mine is."

"Fair point."

A few moments later, the door opened to a bathrobed Nora, scowling and squinting. When I'd first met her, I had dubbed her Sunglasses because she wore these huge, black, wraparound shades. Her eyes were light sensitive.

"Unless you're selling Girl Scout cookies, we don't want any. Oh, and we've already found God, thank you very much."

"It's Andi Steele from the Park Hotel. Don't you remember me?"

She squinted harder, and then her face lit up. "Oh yes, of course. Have you hooked up with the sheriff yet?"

"Ah, no. We're just friends. Remember I told you that?"

She scrunched up her face.

"Who is it?" Kris called from another room.

"It's Andi. From the hotel," Nora shouted over her shoulder.

"Did she hook up with the sheriff yet?" Kris called out.

"Nah, she says they're just friends."

A bark of laughter preceded Kris's response. "That's what I said about Duke, and you know what happened there."

Nora nodded at me, like she was giving me life lessons. "Yup, three kids popped out."

"Well," I said, "there aren't any kids popping out of me any time soon."

"Don't worry, dear. You still have a few good years left." Nora patted my hand. "Now, why are you knocking on our door so late?"

"I was wondering if I could ask you some questions about poisonous plants."

She didn't even bat an eye as she opened the door wide. "Sure, come on in."

I followed her though the cozy living room to the kitchen. She pointed to a chair, and I sat down.

"Do you want some tea?" she asked.

"I'd love some, thank you."

While Nora filled the kettle with water, Kris shuffled into the kitchen. When I'd first met her, I'd nicknamed her Blue, as she wore the brightest blue cardigan I'd ever seen. The bright blue robe she wore now suggested that blue might be her favorite color.

"I hope I'm not disturbing you," I said.

She waved a wrinkled hand at me. "Nonsense. We don't often get visitors, especially at night. It's like living on the edge." She sunk into another chair at the wooden kitchen table.

"Yeah, this is probably as rowdy as we've been in twenty years," Nora added as she plopped tea bags into three cups.

"Speak for yourself," Kris said, "I was at the bingo riot of 2002."

Nora nodded and clucked her tongue. "Oh yeah, that's right."

I glanced at Kris, eyebrow raised. "Bingo riot?"

"Oh, honey, it's a story that would make your jaw drop." She patted my hand on the table. "I'll save it for another time."

Nora set the tea cups on the table and took a seat. "So, what do you need to know about plants?"

"I'm wondering if you knew what plants or flowers are the most poisonous."

Nora shook her head. "You could just ask the Google that question and get an immediate answer. There's lots of poisonous plants. And some are poisonous to pets but not to people. Stuff like that. So, what do you really want to know?"

"What would be the purpose of handling poisonous plants? Why work with them? Doesn't seem logical to me."

"Well, take hemlock, for example," Kris said. "Can be used for different naturopathic treatments for things like asthma. It has been used in the past for pain relief from teething."

"What about the others?"

Nora nodded. "Well, oleander seeds have been used as medicines for heart conditions, and asthma and menstrual cramps even."

"Now, foxglove is a different beast," Kris said. "It shouldn't ever be used in self-healing. There is a chemical compound taken from the foxglove that is used to make the pharmaceutical drug called digoxin, which is used for heart conditions."

"Which poisonous plants would be the best to kill someone?" I asked.

Nora glanced at Kris, who pursed her wrinkled lips. "Foxglove," they said in unison.

"Why?"

"Because it's lethal, and it doesn't take as much to poison," Kris said. "The others would take longer and require a larger amount."

Nora's eyes widened as she stared at me. "You're thinking of that poor mainlander who was found dead in the maze. Hm. Makes sense some kind of plant might have killed her, considering she was a florist. You have to be careful when you're messing around with plants. A lot of people don't realize that. But she should have."

"It's just a theory," I said, but they were smart women and could easily put two and two together.

"Do you want to see what foxglove looks like?" Kris asked. "We have some in the greenhouse. It's a pretty plant."

Five minutes later, we were all crowded in their small greenhouse that was in the back yard. Kris pointed to a three-foot pink column of upside-down bell-type flowers. She was right. They were very pretty. Next to it was another pot of purple ones, and another pot of white ones.

"Is it safe to handle? Can you get a rash on your hands?" I asked as I studied the flowers.

"A person should always wear gloves when handling any plant," Nora said.

Kris nodded. "You could get a rash from the sap the flower produces."

"Do you think someone poisoned that woman?" Nora asked.

"Not sure."

"If I wanted to kill someone, I'd use ricin from the castor bean plant. It would be instantaneous, and you'd need to use only a little," Kris said.

"What if you wanted to kill someone over time? Slowly poison them?"

Kris pursed her lips again. "Oleander or hemlock. Grind up the seeds, sprinkle into something, like food or drink, do it for weeks. That would do the trick. The person wouldn't even know."

I left the sisters with my head full of plant knowledge and promises that I'd consider "getting on the sheriff before he's taken." I cruised around the village pondering what I'd just learned. If June had wanted to kill Brittany, there were other better ways to do it than by poisoning her with plants. For one thing, the amount of poison and the length of time it would take to kill her…it just didn't make sense that June would have gone through all that trouble. She didn't see Brittany socially, since Brittany lived on the mainland. June wouldn't have had a regular opportunity to administer a slow-acting poison. The murderer probably had spent time with Brittany often and on a regular basis. Which meant the killer would have been someone close to her. Like a boyfriend or family member or a coworker, if she'd had any.

In my mind, that put Tyler and Brittany's sister as the most viable suspects. They had means and opportunity, at least. What about motive?

Before I headed off in that direction, I wanted to clear June completely. I parked the golf cart on Market Street right in front of June's Blooms. If she had any of the possible flower killers, they'd likely be in her cold storage. I wasn't sure where June got her flowers—whether she purchased them from a distributor or grew her own. If they came from a distributor, she'd have records of her purchases. If she grew her own, there would be indications of that as well. And now that I knew what I was looking for...

Although it was dark inside, I tried the door to her shop. It was locked, of course. I glanced across the street at the station and wondered if June was still there. Had she been arrested? Or had the dragon lady gotten her released, meaning June was now at home? Either way, I didn't want to bother June.

I took out my phone and called Ginny. "Hey, question...does the hotel happen to have a key to June's shop?"

"No, why?"

"I need to get in to check some stuff out."

"Why don't you just ask June?"

"Because of her pain-in-the-butt lawyer."

"The one you called?" she asked.

"Yes, but I didn't know she was going to freeze me out when I made the call."

"Sorry, my friend. Guess you're going to have to find another way."

I hung up and then stared at the door, wondering how I was going to get in without doing something illegal or unethical.

"You're not planning on breaking in are you?"

His voice startled me, but I didn't turn as the sheriff stepped up beside me.

"No, of course not."

"Good, because then I'd have to arrest you."

"I'm pretty sure you threatened me with that when we first met." I couldn't stop the small grin that spread over my face.

His lips also twitched up. "So, what are you doing here?"

"Trying to prove that June didn't kill Brittany Gervais." I turned toward him. "If poison from a plant was used, there is no way June had the opportunity to do it. She and Brittany disliked each other. They had a falling out at some point, so June only saw Brittany, like, once a year at the Flower Festival. Besides that, June might not even have the possible murder weapon in her possession. With some expert advice, we narrowed the deadly plants down to three possibilities—hemlock, oleander, and foxglove."

He nodded. "The expert I talked to basically said the same thing. Who did you talk to?"

I made a face and wouldn't look at him. "Um, Nora Gray and Kris Houston."

"Your experts are two eighty-year-old women who have often catcalled me from across the street?"

I gave him a look. "You'd be surprised what they know."

"Yeah, I probably would be." He took a step toward the door, took out a key, and unlocked it.

"What are you doing?"

"I have a search warrant." He pulled it out of his jacket pocket and showed it to me.

"Do you know what you're looking for?"

He nodded. "I have an idea what the plants look like."

"Okay, so you can tell the difference between hemlock and yarrow or fennel? And foxglove and comfrey or borage? And sometimes oleander is mistaken for wild roses or St. John's wart."

He stared dumbly at me.

"That's what I thought. Obviously, my experts were more thorough than yours."

He sighed. "Fine. You can come along, but don't touch anything."

"You don't have an extra pair of gloves?" I asked.

"No."

"Good thing I just happened to bring my own, then," I smiled sweetly, reaching into my pocket to pull mine out and glove up.

He entered the shop, and I followed behind. After snapping on his gloves, the sheriff turned on the lights, and we went around the counter to the back of the shop, where both the cold storage and June's office were located.

When we entered the office, Sheriff Jackson went to turn on her computer.

"If you're looking for her orders, they'd be in a filing cabinet. She keeps records of everything on paper."

"How do you know that?"

"She told me, plus everything she does with the hotel has a paper trail. Samuel hates using the computer. Every order from the hotel is hand-delivered to June. I know. I've had to do those deliveries."

The tall metal filing cabinet sat in the corner. Sheriff Jackson opened the first drawer. All the files were listed by date, and there were a lot of them. He pulled out one file and flipped through it.

"I'll have to get a couple of deputies to box up the files and bring them to the station so we can go through them. There's no way I can read them on my own. There's too many." He put the file back and closed the drawer.

"Let's check the cold storage," I said.

The big cooler had a heavy metal door, like a freezer in a restaurant. The sheriff opened it and a waft of cool air hit me in the face. I shivered and followed him in. The large room contained several work tables, shelves of vases and pots, a large sink, and three refrigeration units with glass doors. All her work tools were hanging on one wall—shears, trowels, and others I didn't know the names of.

The sheriff opened one refrigeration unit and scoured the glass shelves. Some of the flowers and plants were tied in bundles. Others were already potted in decorative containers. His eyes narrowed, and he pointed to one shelf where there was a cluster of weed-like plants with tiny white flowers.

"That looks like hemlock," he said.

I shooed him out of the way and peered at the plant. I shook my head. "That's baby's breath, not hemlock."

He closed the door and then opened the next unit. There was nothing in there that jumped out at me as potentially offending plants. As he opened the door of the third unit, I spotted a splash of pink, and my heart slammed into my chest. Slowly, he opened the door and peered inside. He pointed to the pink bell-like flowers.

"Is that foxglove?" he asked.

I came in closer to the flowers, not wanting it to be true. I peered at the stem and leaves and the flowers, and let out the breath I was holding. "Those are snapdragons."

"Are you sure?"

I took out my phone and scrolled through my photos. I showed him a close-up picture of the foxglove growing in Kris and Nora's greenhouse. "This is foxglove. See how the flower is really bell shaped, and see the spots on the inside of the petals?"

"Right." He nodded but then his gaze lifted. "Do they come in other colors?"

"Yeah, purple, white…"

"How about yellow?"

I peered toward the flowers he was pointing at, and my stomach sank.

There were three bunches of pale-yellow foxglove on the second shelf.

Chapter Fifteen

"THIS DOESN'T NECESSARILY MEAN anything," I pointed out. "They are pretty flowers, and she likely uses them in arrangements."

"But it could mean something," he replied. "We can't ignore that she has the plants on hand."

"There's no reason June would kill Brittany, Sheriff. I'm pretty sure June had an affair with Brittany's husband, Simon, five years ago. That's when their friendship ended. Why would June kill her now?" I put my hand up. "And please don't tell me June's motive was this stupid flower-arranging contest. I simply don't believe June would kill Brittany over that, and no one else will believe it, either."

He shrugged. "Dunno. Here's what I do know. Brittany is divorced. Got divorced four years ago. Maybe Simon left Brittany for June but then decided to go back to his wife. That could have made June angry enough to kill."

I still didn't believe it. "Have you found Simon?"

He shook his head. "Nope. I sent a deputy out to his house on the mainland. He wasn't home, and there was a bunch of mail jammed into his mailbox. Like several weeks' worth, maybe more."

"Seems to me you have a missing ex-husband with a motive."

He gave me a look. "What motive?"

"I'm guessing there was life insurance, right?"

"We're looking into it, Andi." He gave me a sincere look. "I know you don't want June to be guilty. Heck, I don't want her to be guilty, but until we solve this case, I have to look at all possibilities."

"Exactly," I said, "which is why you should look into this Tyler guy and Brittany's sister. What was her name?"

"Tracy Hamlin."

"Those two had the means and the opportunity. Much more opportunity than June had."

"Like I said, I'm considering everything and everyone until we find sufficient evidence to make an arrest."

I kept quiet about the two agricultural bioengineers in town looking for Tyler until I could come up with a plausible working theory that tied them to Brittany. The sheriff had procedures and rules to follow, along with investigating Tyler and Brittany's sister. He was also faced with a challenge to make sense of June's paperwork. There were a lot of order forms to go through.

Which meant there were two things I could do to help: find the connection between Tyler, Ackerman Biosystems, and Brittany, and locate Simon.

My phone jingled from my purse. I took it out, saw it was Daniel calling, and answered. "Hey, you."

"Hey back. I found that info you wanted."

"You did? That was fast."

"Maybe it's because I miss you, and now you'll come over."
I turned away from the sheriff. "That's not fair. You know I've been busy."

"And...?"

I could feel the sheriff's inquisitive gaze on me, so I walked outside, pulling off my gloves as I went. "And what? There's no other reason."

"Are you sure?"

"Yes." But my gaze wandered back into the shop to look at Sheriff Jackson. Could it be that my real reason was wearing a hat and a badge?

"What time should I pick you up at the ferry?" Daniel asked.

"Tomorrow around four?" I pushed the gloves into my purse.

"Sounds good. I'm looking forward to it."

"Me too." I disconnected and put the phone back into my purse.

The sheriff had come out of June's shop while I was on the phone. He'd stripped off his gloves and stuffed them into his pocket. "Going to the mainland tomorrow?"

I nodded. "Yep."

"To see Daniel, right? Not to do any unauthorized snooping."

I nodded again. "Yep. To have dinner with Daniel."

He eyed me for a long moment. "You know when you lie, you twitch your nose a little."

My fingers went to my nose. "My nose does not twitch. I would know if it did."

"Don't get me wrong—it's cute as hell, but it's not helpful when you lie to me. Complications arise that can be difficult to deal with, you know?"

Cute as hell? Wow, that's new. I lifted my chin. "Not that it's any of your business, but Daniel is cooking dinner at his place."

He nodded with that judging look on his face. I hated that look. It made me feel both angry and vulnerable, as if he knew there was more danger ahead than he was telling me about.

"And we might even go dancing," I said without thinking. Why did I tell him that? He certainly didn't need to know how I spent my time or who I spent it with.

The muscles along his jawline flinched, and it looked like he was grinding his teeth. "Great." He rubbed at his chin. "Have an enjoyable evening."

I gaped at him as he turned on his boot heel and stomped back into the shop. He pulled his phone from his back pocket and made a call.

I jumped into the cart and drove down Market Street. I turned over the conversation, chastising myself for saying what I had. The sheriff made me so angry sometimes, and I was normally an even-keeled person. I let him push my buttons, which was not necessary. And why in the hell did I care what he thought?

The answer hit me like the bite of a scorpion. Fast, unexpected, and dangerous.

I liked Sheriff Luke Jackson. I liked him a lot. *Damn.*

As I turned right onto Lilac Street, I slowed down and thought about stopping at Chocolat and indulging in a box of salted caramels to temper my anger or frustration or whatever it was. But I'd noticed my expanding waistline lately, so I pressed on. While I was stopped at the corner of Main Street, a man carrying a bag of Chinese takeout rushed across the street in front of my cart.

I recognized him from the one time I'd seen him in the maze. He'd crossed my path in the maze mere minutes before I found Brittany's body. The sheriff wouldn't share any of the witness statements, so I'd simply get one myself. I wanted to know if he'd seen anyone else in the maze, because Brittany must have been meeting someone there that day. The same someone who killed her, if I had any luck at all.

I pulled over quickly, parked the cart, and jumped out. "Hey!" I called to him.

He stopped and looked at me. His eyes widened, and then he turned and booked it in the opposite direction. Why was he running from me?

I was wearing the comfy flats that I usually wore to work, so I chased after him. He dashed down Lilac Street and over to Market. He was a lot quicker than I was, so I lost him when he sprinted into the heavily treed park near the historical society building.

I hadn't had a decent workout in months. By the time I stopped running, I was breathing heavily. There was a stitch in my side, and I massaged it as I peered into the park, trying to figure out where the man had run to and where he was going. Past the park, on the opposite side of Clover Lane, was a small residential area and the road that lead out of the main village and wound along the coastline to a new housing development.

I was pretty sure that June lived in a small bungalow in that residential area off Clover Lane. Coincidence? Possibly.

While I collected my breath, I considered why the guy might have run from me. He'd probably recognized me from the maze that day. Maybe he hadn't been part of the relay race. Now that I thought about it, I hadn't recognized him as an employee of the hotel. Not that I knew every hotel staff member. There were seasonal, temporary, and part-time staff that I didn't know well. He could've been one of the bellhops on the relay team with Ginny. But then why would he run away from me? Something wasn't right.

As I walked back to my cart, I called Ginny. When she answered, there was a lot of background noise. A gaggle of people talking and glasses rattling.

"Where are you?" I asked.

"Swan Song bar. I'm having a drink with Clinton." She paused, and then her voice went up an octave. "You should come down. It's five-dollar drafts for a while longer."

"No, I'm good. What about Barrington from Hong Kong?"

She giggled, but offered no answer. Which I took to mean that she didn't want to discuss Barrington in front of Clinton.

I moved on to the reason for my call. "I have a question, though."

"Shoot."

"Who was the fifth person on your relay team?"

"What?"

"At the festival relay race through the maze. Your team consisted of Eric, Tina, Randy, and another one of the bellhops…"

"Oh, yes. Ollie."

"What does he look like?"

I didn't have to see her to know she was wrinkling her nose as she considered the question. "Average height and weight, I guess. He's definitely not tall or anything. Not a big guy, either."

"Dark hair?"

"No, blond."

"Okay, thanks Ginny. I'll see you later." I hung up and then jumped into the cart.

I turned right onto Main Street with the intention of driving back to the hotel. It was past eight, and I was hungry and tired and maybe a little cranky, too. Instead, I took a right into the alleyway and cut across to Market Street. I drove past Blossom the clothing store and then June's Blooms. The sheriff was still there along with Deputy Shawn, who walked out of the shop just as I cruised by. I continued up past the park near the historical society building.

I drove over Clover Lane and into the residential area, which consisted of about fifteen houses, all of them cute bungalows built long ago. I parked in front of June's pretty pale-green house with the bright-yellow door. The color scheme should've been tacky, but it suited June.

I didn't know if she would talk to me. Her lawyer, Paige, would've instructed her not to talk to anyone about the case. But I had to try, because a lot of things just weren't looking good for her, and Lois had made it clear that she was relying on me to fix this.

Lights were on in the house, so someone was probably home. I knocked on the door and waited. I heard some commotion, possibly chairs moving, and then I saw June's face peering out from behind the floral curtain hanging on the window beside the door. I smiled and waved, friendly like.

A few seconds later, the door opened a crack, and June filled the space. "Hey, Andi."

"Hi, June. How are you?"

"I'm okay, considering."

"I'm glad to hear that. Lois and everyone at the Park will be, too." I paused for breath. "Can I come in?"

She hesitated, and I wondered if it was because of Paige's warning or something else.

"You know I'm on your side, June," I said reassuringly, adding a gentle smile. "Lois insisted that I help you in any way I can. You know how important it is to me not to disappoint Lois."

She worried at her bottom lip with her teeth for a few moments and then finally opened the door for me. I came in, and she led me to the cozy living room. There were plants everywhere, of course. A bookshelf stuffed with books and various candles and knicknacks made the place even more homey. The hunter-green sofa had a multi-colored crocheted afghan tossed over the back. It was all very grandmother-chic.

I perched on the sofa, and June sat on the edge of the easy chair, her back rigid. "What would you like to know?" she asked.

"I found out that you and Brittany had been friends once."

She nodded. "A long time ago. We went to college together. I told the sheriff all of this."

"Did you tell him about Simon?"

She flinched at that. "What do you mean?"

"Wasn't the reason you and Brittany stopped being friends all about Simon?"

She frowned. "Of course not. We fell out over the usual things women do."

"Which are?"

"I don't know. I can't remember why. It just happened."

I didn't want to accuse her of having an affair with Simon. Especially if it wasn't true. I didn't have any proof, just a guess based on that comment from Brittany's sister, Tracy. Which could've been nothing more than ill-will. I considered asking more questions about Simon, but she already seemed on edge and I didn't want to upset her even more.

I also wanted to ask her about the foxglove in her flower storage, but I figured the sheriff would never tell me another thing in confidence if I did. Although I didn't believe for a second that June had murdered Brittany, I wouldn't hamper the course of the investigation. Sheriff Jackson was following the facts. That's exactly what he was supposed to do. That left me free to follow my instincts.

While I thought about more questions to ask, a gray tabby jumped onto the back of the sofa. It started to purr when I reached over to pet it. "Oh, what a sweetie. What's his name?"

"His name is Ash," June replied in a friendlier way than anything she'd said to me so far.

I petted his little head. "Hello, Ash. You're so handsome, aren't you?

He meowed as if to say, "Yes, I am devilishly handsome." Which, of course, he was.

June got to her feet. "If you don't mind, I'd really like to get some sleep. It's been a long and trying day."

I stood. "I'm sorry. I won't take up any more of your time." I petted the cat's head again and then moved toward the front door. As I passed the kitchen, I got a whiff of hot food. "I didn't realize I'd interrupted your dinner."

"Don't worry. It's fine." She opened the door for me.

I walked out. "Thanks, June. Get some sleep."

She closed the door behind me. As I walked down the steps from the door to my cart, I knew June hadn't been totally straight with me. The smell I had caught from the kitchen was Chinese. It had that aroma. I suspected that the mystery man I'd been chasing was dining with June and had brought her Chinese takeout.

I'd seen her cat, Ash, before as well. In the wedding pictures of Simon and Brittany Gervais.

So, it wasn't a huge leap to guess that the man I'd seen in the maze, and running from me on the street, was none other than Brittany's ex, Simon Gervais.

CHAPTER SIXTEEN

AFTER A HORRIBLE FITFUL sleep full of inappropriate dreams about the sheriff, I basically zombie-walked through the next day at the desk. Thankfully, the hotel wasn't busy. I didn't have to deal with too many people, and the majority of them were pleasant. I had only one head-scratcher. A disgruntled man who asked me to rearrange the furniture in his suite to match his astrological sign because his bed needed to face southward. The best I could do for him was to find a room that had a bed facing south. He was satisfied and thanked me in the end, but he'd been most unpleasant about the situation for a while.

During my break, I'd called the sheriff to tell him about about June and Simon but got his voicemail. I left a message then I called the station, but Deputy Shawn told me the sheriff was too busy to talk to me. I told Shawn to let the sheriff know I'd called and it was important. He never called back. Either Shawn never gave him the message or Sheriff Jackson was being a stubborn ass about our little…disagreement the night before.

Once my shift was over, I walked down to the ferry dock to catch the boat over to the mainland. I was excited to see Daniel, but mostly because of the information he'd learned about Brittany's business. He was a great guy—intelligent, successful, fit, and drop-dead gorgeous. So, what was my problem? Any woman should be stoked to be dating him. Why wasn't I?

Daniel was waiting for me when the ferry docked. I perked up a bit when I saw him in the parking lot. My body definitely reacted to him, so maybe all I needed was more time to really get to know him. We'd only had a handful of real dates.

He hugged me when I got to his car, and I inhaled his woodsy scent. "How was the trip?"

"Uneventful, thankfully."

He chuckled and gave me a quick kiss. "Good to hear. I hope you brought your appetite, because I'm making pasta and garlic bread."

"Sounds fabulous. I love any type of pasta."

He opened the door for me, and I slid into the soft leather seat of his BMW. He got in, and we pulled out of the parking lot. I hadn't been to the mainland enough to know the layout of downtown Frontenac City, but I did know that Brittany's shop wasn't that far from the ferry dock.

"Could we drive by Gervais Flower Boutique?"

His eyes narrowed. "Why?"

"Curiosity."

He gave me a disapproving look but didn't press the matter. "Okay."

We drove down the main street in town, and Daniel parked in front of Brittany's shop. I got out and peered through the closed door. It was dark inside because the shop was closed. I wasn't sure what I was looking for. Daniel joined me at the door.

"I have the info you requested at home, but her business was in financial trouble."

"Really?"

He nodded. "She'd taken out a second loan from the bank not long ago."

Peering through the window again, I asked. "Wasn't she the only florist in town?"

"I don't know."

"Was there a co-owner on the business?"

"Yes, actually. Simon Gervais. Her husband, I presume. They started the business together seven years ago."

"Ex-husband," I said. "I'm pretty sure he had an affair with June, who used to be Brittany's best friend."

"Huh," he said with a grin. "The plot thickens."

"It does indeed." I looked down the line of shops. "Is there an alley behind these shops?"

"Yeah."

I started down the sidewalk, toward the intersecting road. Daniel had to take a couple extra steps to catch up to me.

"What are you looking for?" he asked.

"Not sure yet."

We ducked down the alleyway, and I counted back doors until we reached Brittany's shop. It looked the same as all the others. There was no extra building or extension. Daniel must've noticed my frown.

"I'm going to bet that you *do* know what you're looking for."

"Do you know if Brittany ordered in her flowers or if she grew them herself?"

"That's not something I can access as mayor. I have her incorporation papers and business license and her annual reports, and that's it. Oh, and some financials, since she had to include them with her applications."

"So, would you have her home address on those documents?"

"Andi, I'm not driving by Brittany's house." He crossed his arms over his chest. "This really is a police matter. Let them do their job."

I sighed and then nodded. "You're right. It's just sometimes the sheriff is so damn frustrating." I clenched my hands. "He makes me want to pull my hair out."

Narrowing his eyes, Daniel uncrossed his arms and shoved his hands into his pockets. "Yes, I've noticed that."

I had a feeling he wasn't talking about the case. He didn't look all that impressed right now. I moved toward him and slid my hand through the crook of his elbow.

"I'm hungry." I tucked against him. "I'm looking forward to watching you cook dinner for me."

He shook his head a little and then chuckled. "Don't think you just get to watch. You are definitely helping."

"I'm not sure you want me to do that. I'm a bit useless in the kitchen."

"Nothing too hard. Just cutting up some veggies for a salad."

I smiled. "That I can do. I'm pretty handy with a knife."

Daniel's place was a newer three-bedroom house with a big back deck and landscaped back yard. He used one of the bedrooms as an office. The other was a guest bedroom that he told me was often used by his younger brother when he roared into town. The house was built by Daniel's own construction company, which was operated by his dad and his older sister since he'd become mayor.

Inside, the place was beautifully decorated. A bit too minimalist for my taste, but it was neat and tidy, much like the man who lived there. The only bit of decorating chaos belonged to his dog, Max, a golden retriever with a big personality. I fell in love with him the second he jumped up and licked my hand after trying desperately to lick my face.

The conversation was light and fun as we made dinner together. We talked about crazy stories from college. I didn't have too many to share because I'd been pretty tame in school, although I did amuse him with stories about what my classmates had done. Daniel's shenanigans weren't too wild, either. Just the average amount of college-boy antics. A little drinking, a few harmless pranks, and the time he backed out of streaking across the football field at the very last second, but his friend did it anyway and made the local news. Daniel laughed and said he was lucky he had backed out because his opponent would have made a big deal about it during his campaign for mayor.

After a delicious meal of spinach tomato tortellini and the green salad I clumsily assembled, we did the dishes together. Once I finished the last pot and put it into the rack to dry, Daniel took the dish cloth from me, draped it over the faucet, and moved closer.

Nerves zipped through me as I took a step backward, my back hitting the counter. He leaned in for a kiss.

But I couldn't. Not when thoughts of Sheriff Jackson invaded my mind.

Daniel sensed my reluctance. He sighed and pulled back to look at me. "What's wrong?"

"Nothing." I sighed as well.

"But?"

"I'm sorry, Daniel. I'm just not ready for this."

He took stepped away and leaned against the island. "Is it the sheriff?"

I made a face, scrunched up my mouth. "No?"

He nodded. "Andi, I really like you—"

"I like you, too."

"And I'll be patient. But I won't wait forever."

"I wouldn't expect you to." I reached for him and squeezed his hand. "I think you're amazing, Daniel. I do."

He gave me a small, quick smile. "I'll drive you back to the ferry. It's getting late."

The drive to the dock was quiet. Daniel only spoke a few words when I asked him a question. I knew he was disappointed with how the evening had turned out. The conflicted feelings I had for Sheriff Jackson stood in the way. I sensed he knew that was the problem, which didn't help matters any.

After he parked in the lot, he handed me a manila envelope. "Here's all the info I could get on Brittany Gervais's business."

"Thank you, Daniel, I really appreciate it."

"Just stay out of trouble, Andi, please. You worry me."

"I will, I promise. It's not like I'm reckless. I'm just doing a little investigating for June's sake. That's all." I gave him a reassuring smile.

"Okay. Goodnight."

I leaned over the console and gave him a soft kiss. "Goodnight." I opened the car door and got out.

Once I had my ticket in hand, Daniel drove out of the parking lot. I waved, and then he was gone. While I waited for the ferry to take on passengers, I opened the envelope and slid out the contents. I flipped quickly through the incorporation papers. Nothing nefarious or odd jumped out at me, except that, yes, there was Simon Gervais's name listed as co-owner of Gervais Flower Boutique.

The financials for Brittany's business revealed what Daniel had mentioned about the overspending and insufficient revenue to pay back the initial loan she'd needed to start the company. Another loan had been obtained by Brittany herself without Simon, it looked like.

As I skimmed over the pages, my gaze landed on her home address—345 Lakeside Lane. I suspected her home was probably close to the shop and the town center. I could've been wrong since the town was three times the size of Frontenac Village. But it made sense to me that if there was something to find, her house was a good place to start.

The call to board the ferry came over the loudspeaker, and the line of people in front of me started to move forward. I moved with the flow, but then I glanced over at the parking lot and spotted an empty taxi. It was only seven thirty. I could go to Brittany's home, come back, and still catch the last ferry at nine.

I stepped out of line and ran toward the taxi, waving my arm. No one needed to know about my brief detour. It would be my secret.

CHAPTER SEVENTEEN

IT TOOK ONLY TEN minutes to reach the residential address listed on Brittany's business forms. I paid the driver and got out to stand on the sidewalk in front of the small, darkened house. Lights blazed from every other house on the block. A surge of sadness swelled over me because Brittany wouldn't be turning on the lights in her little house again.

I wasn't one hundred percent sure what I was doing here. I had no intention of breaking into her house. But I did want to see if she had a greenhouse. There was a connection to Tyler and Ackerman Biosystems somewhere, and I was determined to find it.

As I walked across the lawn toward the back of the house, I went over the conversation between Tyler and Brittany that I'd overheard. At first, I'd thought it was a quarrel between lovers, but the more I considered the words and how they were conveyed, it could've easily been an argument between friends, maybe even coworkers. And Brittany's sister and Tyler had acted pretty familiar with each other, too. Tracy seemed more than just a friend to her sister's distraught boyfriend, anyway. Maybe it was Tracy and Tyler who had been lovers, and not Brittany and Tyler. If that was the case, why were Tyler and Brittany hanging out together?

The distant barking of a dog startled me a little as I crept along the fence separating Brittany's property from her neighbor's. When I came around the corner of the house, there it was—a greenhouse. It was a large glass structure that took up most of the back yard.

I walked toward the building, glad there were no streetlights shining into the yard which might have allowed the neighbors to see me. I was about to reach for the handle to the side door of the greenhouse, when a flash of light nearly blinded me. I dropped down to my knees, smashing my right knee onto a pile of bricks. Biting down on my lip to stifle my grunting pain, I peered through the glass to see where the beam of light had come from. The beam swept over the top of my head. Seemed like a flashlight inside the greenhouse.

Silently, I debated whether to call the police. That was the smart thing to do, but whoever it was might easily get away before the police could arrive. I wanted to know who was rummaging around inside. The sound of clay pots knocking against each other resounded from beyond the glass. Then something fell and shattered on the ground. The intruder was looking for something. Casual thieves didn't break into a greenhouse to steal house plants.

I moved closer and crouched next to the door. I wrapped my hand around the handle and slowly pulled the door open. Then I jumped up and dashed inside the greenhouse. My sudden arrival startled the intruder. More pots crashed to the floor. The beam from the flashlight swung around and shined directly into my eyes. Momentarily blinded, my eyes closed reflexively, and I stumbled to the side. Big hands shoved me hard to the ground.

I reached out, flailed around, and grabbed a jeans-covered leg. He kicked out and shook me off roughly, with a grunt. I managed to grab something out of his hands. I fell to the ground again, clutching what felt like paper, just as red and blue strobe lights swept over the yard.

I folded the paper and shoved it into my pants just as a man filled the open doorway of the greenhouse, holding a heavy mag flashlight in one hand and a gun in another. "Sheriff's Department. Don't move."

I put my hands up. "I'm unarmed."

"Stand up," the Frontenac City deputy ordered.

I did, and he shined the light in my face. Then he lowered his gun and holstered it. I guess I must've exhibited an innocent look. I certainly didn't look like a criminal. He demanded, "What are you doing here?"

"I heard someone rummaging around in the greenhouse and came to take a look."

"You heard that from the street?"

I pressed my lips together. "Um, yes. It was loud."

He cocked his head. "Uh-huh. And why are you here at this residence? I know you don't live here. I know…I mean, I knew the woman who lived here."

"Right. Well, I'm from the Park Hotel, where Ms. Gervais's body was found, and—"

"And you thought you'd come by here to satisfy your morbid curiosity, is that it?" he said.

"No. Not at all. I thought maybe I could help find out what happened to her."

"By destroying her property?" He swung the light around the broken pots and ruined plants on the ground.

Squinting, I spotted white and red flowers that could've come from the oleander bush, but could've easily have been wild roses, too.

"I told you I heard someone in here. I'm not the one who did this."

"Then who did?"

"I don't know. He ran off right before you showed up. You didn't see a man running away from the house?"

"No, I didn't." The deputy looked at me. "All I see is you, with dirt on your pants and your hands."

"Would you believe I fell?"

The look he gave me told me that he didn't believe that for a minute.

"Look, Deputy, this is all just a big misunderstanding."

"Show me some ID," he said, not backing down.

"Okay." I dusted the dirt off my hands and opened my purse, which was slung across my chest, and took out my wallet. I opened it and handed it to him.

He took it and shined the light onto my driver's license. "Andrea Steele?"

"My parents liked ABBA."

He frowned at me, and I realized maybe he was too young to even know who ABBA was. "Your address is in Sacramento."

"Yes, I moved to Frontenac Island a few months ago."

"Then why does it say Sacramento?"

"Because I haven't gotten it changed yet."

"Why not?"

That was a good question. I could've told him because I was holding on to the slim hope that I'd be cleared of all suspicion in my boss's embezzlement scheme and immediately return to sunny, warm California to practice law. But I didn't want to say I was living under a cloud of suspicion for a worse crime than breaking into a backyard greenhouse.

I took a breath. "I guess I was waiting until my license expired, and I had a more permanent address so I could get it all done in one swoop."

"You don't have a permanent address? That makes you a vagrant," he said.

Seriously? Did I look like a homeless person? "Well, I live at the Park Hotel. I'm not a vagrant. Not at all."

His eyes narrowed, and he handed my wallet back. "Okay, let's take a drive down to the station."

"Couldn't you just let me go?" I smiled and batted my eyelashes in an unabashed display of flirtation.

"No." He wasn't moved by my flirting. Not even a little bit. I must have been losing my touch.

He put me in the back seat of his cruiser. It wasn't the first time I'd been in a cop's car. I went on a ride-along with Sacramento's finest once. It was an eye-opening experience. We responded to three separate domestic-abuse calls and a trespassing complaint. But the most eye-popping incident was a drunk and disorderly after a very tall and muscular drag queen threw her size 12 stiletto into a group of rude college boys who were catcalling her. One of the boys caught the heel on his forehead, and it drew blood. We all figured he deserved it. The officers let her go.

When we got to the station, Deputy Frank Nelson (I could read his name tag once we were inside), marched me in and told me to sit in a chair by his desk. He said he wasn't booking me or anything, for which I was grateful. That wouldn't have helped out with my California legal troubles at all. But he was going to take my statement and make my night miserable. I'd miss the last ferry back to Frontenac Island, for sure. And that meant I'd be late for work tomorrow. Which would be another whole can of worms. So I asked if I could make a call. He allowed it.

The phone rang only twice before he picked up.

"Hey. So, I did something I promised I wouldn't do." I heard him groan. "Can you come get me?"

CHAPTER EIGHTEEN

LESS THAN AN HOUR later, my savior walked into the station, his face a stern mask. I got to my feet and walked over to him.

"Thanks for coming, Sheriff."

He looked me over, his eyes narrowing when he noticed my torn pants. They'd ripped at the knee when I'd been pushed to the ground. "Are you okay?"

I nodded. "A couple of scratches. Nothing serious."

He looked over my shoulder at the deputy. "Any charges here, Frank?"

"Nah. I think she got more than she bargained for while trespassing. I know where to find her when the owner wants to be reimbursed for the damages. Meanwhile, I don't want to deal with all that paperwork," Deputy Nelson replied.

"I wasn't really trespassing, Deputy." Although, I was, clearly. I had no idea how I'd pay for the damages to the greenhouse and its contents. Which meant I'd need to find the real culprit.

"Don't push your luck," the sheriff grumbled low under his breath. Then to Deputy Nelson, "Thanks. Have a good night, Frank."

"You too, Luke."

I turned and waved at the deputy. "'Night."

He shook his head and returned his attention to the mound of paperwork on his desk.

Giving me another stern look, Sheriff Jackson walked out of the station. I had to rush to catch up. When we reached his sedan, he opened the passenger door for me. I jumped in, and he shut it, and then came around to get into the driver's side.

The second he pulled out of the lot, he twisted to glare at me. "What the hell were you doing? I thought you were having dinner with Daniel."

"Don't get your boxers in bunch," I said a little defensively. "I had a suspicion that things weren't all that peachy in Brittany's world, and I was right. Her company is having money troubles. And I found out that her ex-husband, Simon, is still part owner. I think it has something to do with plant genetics."

"Plant genetics?" he said, eyebrows arched.

"Yup. I overheard two guys, one a bioengineer from Ackerman Biosystems, talking at the Park Hotel. They are on the island looking for Tyler. I'm not sure what he's done, or how he's connected, but I did manage to grab this before the guy in the greenhouse shoved me to the ground. I think it was probably Tyler, by the way." I reached into my pants, and the sheriff's eyes widened as I pulled out a folded piece of paper. I unfolded it and handed it to him.

I'd already taken a peek at it when I excused myself to go to the restroom back at the Frontenac City sheriff's office. I wasn't one hundred percent sure what it was, but the writing was definitely chemical formulas of some sort. My best guess was that Brittany and Tyler were playing around with plant DNA. It looked like they'd been mixing various plants and recording the results. For what purpose, I didn't know for sure, but it seemed likely the formulas had some connection to Ackerman Biosystems.

Sheriff Jackson looked at the formulas on the paper, his frown deepening. "What am I looking at?"

"Chemical compound equations."

"For what?"

"I don't know, but they were playing around with certain plants. Some of the plants are highly toxic. Maybe they were making something dangerous, and someone from Ackerman killed Brittany over it. Or maybe Tyler killed her to keep something secret."

He made a humming noise. I recognized it as his *I'm considering what you are saying but not quite buying it* sound.

He folded up the paper and slid it into his pocket. I was going to argue with him about it, as I'd found the paper and had plans of my own for using it. But since he had bailed me out, I figured I'd better not push my luck. Besides, I'd taken photos of the document with my phone when I first examined it myself.

"You don't have a lot of faith in me, do you? I knew about Brittany's financial issues. I pulled her bank statements," Sheriff Jackson said, still frowning. "There was a lot of money going out of her account. I also knew Simon was the co-owner of Brittany's business."

I'd considered telling the sheriff that I thought I'd found Simon, who'd been shacking up with June, but that would look bad for her. I wanted time to make sure that what I'd seen, or assumed, was true first. I really hoped I'd made a mistake. I hoped even more that we weren't all wrong about June. And that she wasn't responsible for Brittany's death.

But the circumstantial evidence against June was stacking up. I wasn't sure what to believe, and I knew how important it was to remain objective. I'd placed too much faith in my old boss, and it had cost me everything. I wouldn't make that mistake again.

CHAPTER NINETEEN

THE FERRY RIDE OVER from the mainland to Frontenac Island was pretty quiet. I'd moved up to stand on the top deck to enjoy the view. But the sheriff went to find a quiet spot to make some calls. I didn't think he wanted to talk to me anyway. Luke Jackson wore his anger, disappointment, and annoyance with me on his sleeve.

When we docked on the island, the sheriff offered me a ride, and I accepted. When he pulled up in front of the hotel to drop me off, he asked, "Who did you surprise inside the greenhouse?"

I guess he'd tired of waiting for me to volunteer the information. "I don't know. I didn't see his face. I don't think he was a very big man. His legs were pretty skinny."

He frowned.

"I grabbed his leg. It was thin," I explained.

He nodded. "If you were forced to guess…"

"Then I'd guess Tyler."

"Why?"

"He keeps coming up, doesn't he?" I shrugged. "He's connected to Brittany and to this biosystems company. So he'd know where Brittany lived. He'd know she had the greenhouse and probably what was inside. Maybe they were making something they shouldn't have been."

"Like what?" he asked, his eyes narrowed. I liked that he was taking me seriously and not shrugging off what I had to say. Early on in our uneasy partnership, he hadn't wanted to hear anything I might suggest.

"New plant species maybe?" I chewed on my cuticle, thinking. "Brittany was in financial trouble. Maybe she employed Tyler and they were working together on something new that they could sell. Maybe to the biosystems company."

"And what about the ex, Simon? How does he fit in?"

I shrugged, trying to keep my gaze level. "Maybe he doesn't."

But I believed he did. Maybe he didn't kill Brittany, but he would definitely have known something was going on. Maybe he was in on it, or maybe he wanted a piece of the potentially lucrative pie. He owned part of the company, and he would be responsible for the debts as well. Was June covering for him? Was she an accessory to murder?

The sheriff frowned and narrowed his gaze. "Are you telling me all the facts?"

I scrunched my face into mock indignation, which was the best I could do. He'd asked about the facts, not my educated guesses. So I replied truthfully, "Yes, of course."

"Okay, I'm going to bring Tyler in again. See if he has an alibi for tonight."

"Thanks for believing me."

He looked me straight in the face. "Of course, I believe you. Why wouldn't I?"

We stared at each other for a long uncomfortable moment over the console separating us, and then he cleared his throat and settled back into his seat. "I've got to go."

"Er, right." I opened the door. "Thanks for picking me up."

He nodded, then as I slid out of the car, he said, "Andi?"

"Yeah?"

He licked his lips and then gave a sharp shake of his head. "There's a killer out there. Don't get into any more trouble, okay?"

"I'll try not to." I shut the door, and he slowly pulled away from the curb.

I was able to make it to my suite without being intercepted by anyone who needed something. I also didn't want to answer questions about why I looked like a homeless person, since my clothes were dirty and torn, and my hair had escaped from its ponytail during my scuffle with the greenhouse burglar. Living in the luxurious hotel I worked for had its advantages, like free room and board, amazing food, and access to the pool and fitness center. But privacy and downtime was rare indeed. I had to get serious about finding a place to rent in the village. On top of everything else, I really missed my cats.

While I changed out of my ruined clothes, I started a bath. It would feel good to soak my sore knee and hands. I grabbed the bathtub caddy and positioned it across the tub. The caddy was a clever thing I picked up at one of the shops in the village. It had a slot for a wineglass and holders for candles and a tea cup. It also had a groove in the wood that could be used to set up an electronic device for reading or web surfing or email and texting. I used it the old-fashioned way, though. I put a notebook and pen on the wood surface. After I added lavender-scented salts to the tub, I sunk into the hot, silky water with a long groan of pleasure.

As I soaked, I made a list of the things I knew and things I needed to find out:

1. Brittany Gervais was poisoned according to ME
2. June's pink gardening gloves were found at the scene (she claims they were stolen)
3. Last person to possibly see Brittany alive was Simon Gervais, ex-husband, who is also co-owner of the flower boutique and maybe June's lover.
4. Brittany's company's in debt; large withdrawals from bank account.
5. Something transpired between Simon and June, which caused a rift between Brittany and June (affair?)
6. Brittany and June had a five-year-long feud over the Flower Festival floral award.
7. June doesn't have a solid alibi for the time of Brittany's death.
8. June does possess foxglove, which is a poisonous flower that can cause death and might have been the cause here.
9. Tyler and Brittany argued on the day she died.
10. Tyler and Brittany may have been working together on some project (What? Possible plant development)
11. Tyler is possibly involved with Tracy (Brittany's sister)
12. Two bioengineers are on the island looking for Tyler (Why?)
13. Tyler (maybe) removed something (evidence?) from Brittany's greenhouse. Were there oleander flowers there?

I put the pen down and leaned back in the tub, closing my eyes and allowing the water to slosh up to my neck. I dipped my hands into the water and rubbed them over my face, letting the water's heat soothe my tired, sore muscles.

There was a lot I was missing. Where was the money going? Why was Ackerman Biosystems interested in Tyler? Was there a connection between the engineers and whatever was going on in Brittany's greenhouse? Was Simon involved in everything? Had he planned to profit, but something went wrong? Did Simon use June's botanical skills to create a poison to kill Brittany?

Looking at my list again, it seemed like one giant conspiracy that involved everyone. But giant conspiracies rarely existed. Most often, Occam's Razor applied. One should not make more assumptions than the minimum needed. The simplest, easiest answer was usually the correct one.

I closed my eyes and sank under the water again until just my nose stuck out, like a snorkel tube. I took in some deep breaths, relaxing my body from my toes to my head. The sound of my phone vibrating brought me up.

I reached over the tub for my towel, wiped my hand, and then picked up my phone to see a text from an unknown phone number.

I need to talk to you.

I texted back: *Who is this?*

A friend of June's. Meet me at the fountain ASAP.

I texted: *Is this Simon? Did you get my number from June?*

I waited, but no texts came back.

I set my phone on the caddy and climbed out of the tub. My entire body felt like one big limp noodle. After toweling off quickly, I dressed in leggings and a baggy top. I put my hair up into a messy bun and slipped my feet into a pair of running shoes.

Briefly, I allowed myself to wonder whether I really was going to meet some anonymous texter in the middle of the night. Of course I was. I could defend myself. And this wasn't a dangerous spy mission or anything.

The texter was probably Simon Gervais, because he'd said he was a friend of June's. Seeing me chasing him today must've rattled him.

I wouldn't be unarmed, either. I had a can of pepper spray in my purse. Ginny had given it to me because of the last time I went chasing after a guy alone in the dark. Besides all of that, it wasn't late enough that I'd be the only one out in the gardens. Guests frequently went for nighttime walks through the fairy-lighted trees and bushes.

When I arrived at the fountain, there were a few couples meandering along the garden paths. I sat on the edge of the stone basin, vigilantly watching the shadows for my mysterious texter. I took out my phone and texted: *I'm here.*

After about fifteen minutes, I considered that my anonymous friend had chickened out. And then I spotted a man stepping out from behind the huge topiary bush trimmed to look like a swan. The closer he came, the more recognizable he became. He was indeed the man I'd seen in the maze, the one who'd run from me on the street. He hadn't changed much from his wedding photos. Brittany's ex-husband, Simon Gervais. June Biddle's secret lover.

His gaze darted all over the garden. "I thought you might call the sheriff."

"I didn't think I had reason to. Yet." I stood as he approached. I didn't want to be at a tactical disadvantage. "What did you want to talk to me about, Simon?"

His eyebrows popped up but he nodded. "Yeah, I thought you might have figured that out."

"You need to go talk to the sheriff. You may have been the last person to see Brittany alive."

"You assume I killed her, then?"

"Did you?" I asked. My hand slid into my pocket and wrapped around the pepper spray.

"No." He rubbed at the back of his neck. "I did see her, though."

He paced as he spoke, as if he needed the activity to lay out his logic. "She asked me to meet her in the maze. It was an ironic and bitter choice because that was where she caught me kissing June the first time. She wanted to make an impression. Brittany was like that. Always making points. Showing she was superior."

"Why did she want to meet with you?"

"She didn't. Meeting her was my request. She just picked the spot." He rubbed his neck again. "We were divorced but still connected by her floral business. I wanted to tell her that I was done and that she could buy me out. I wanted a clean break from her."

"You were planning to marry June."

He nodded. "I proposed to her a couple months back."

"What happened?"

His pacing increased, and sweat beaded his brow. "Brittany said she couldn't afford to buy me out. Not right now. If I held on for another few months, she said she could pay me double."

"What did she mean? How could she pay you double in a few short months?"

"I don't know. But she didn't look good. She was sweaty and pale. She kept swiping at the air as if there was a bee trying to sting her. That's when I noticed the pink gloves she was wearing. They belonged to June. I knew that because I bought them for her."

I nodded. At least the mystery of the garden gloves was solved. "But why was Brittany wearing June's gloves?"

"I didn't have a chance to ask her. I don't know."

"Then what did Brittany do?"

"She babbled on a bit about changing the world." He shrugged. "I told her I wanted out now, so I could move on with June. She tore off the gloves, balled them up, and threw them at me, telling me I could go to hell. She had quite a temper, and I knew I couldn't reason with her until she had a chance to cool off. So I left."

I said, "And that's when I ran into you."

He nodded again. "I swear that Brittany was alive when I left her."

I looked at him for a long moment. He was definitely agitated, but I believed his story. "Why did you contact me?"

"Because I know you don't think June killed Brittany, and I'm afraid they're going to charge her with murder."

"Why do you think that?"

But his attention had been drawn by something over my shoulder. His eyes widened, and he turned and ran.

"Simon!"

I twisted around to see what he'd been looking at, but there was nothing there. Shadows. I squinted harder. Moving shadows. I walked toward the trees, pulling the pepper spray out of my pocket on the way.

When I reached the clump of trees, I didn't find anyone lying in wait to jump out at me. Only air and leaves and fairy lights. I turned to go back to the hotel, when I noticed a cigarette butt glowing on the path. I crouched and picked it up. The end was still smoldering, and the oddly sweet smell of smoke filled my nostrils.

CHAPTER TWENTY

FOR THE REST OF the night, I thought about what Simon had
told me and the possibility someone had been watching us.
Simon had definitely been scared of something. There was more
to this tale than he let on. I believed he hadn't killed Brittany.
He'd been straightforward about that much. But I suspected he
knew what she and Tyler were up to.

He must have known Brittany's business was in trouble.
He'd most likely have discussed it with Brittany, because her
financials records showed the problems existed for months. A
year is a long time to not know a business Simon had invested
heavily in was experiencing money trouble.

When I returned to my suite, I had secured the chain lock on
my door and put the steel rod in place on the balcony door. I
didn't sleep with the lights on, but I'd been tempted. Whoever
had been watching us was probably there because of Simon. But
after Simon talked with Brittany in the maze, she'd ended up
dead. Killers tended to repeat the same methods, especially when

those methods had been successful. If our watcher tonight was the same guy who killed Brittany, he might come after me next.

I'd tried texting and calling the number Simon had used to contact me, but got nowhere. Maybe it had been a disposable phone, and he'd already tossed it away. I wanted to talk to June. She could convince Simon to talk to the sheriff.

In the morning, I called Lois to see if she could get someone to cover the desk for me.

"You're making a habit of this, Andi. If you're not careful, Samuel will get the idea that the Park doesn't even need one concierge, let alone two," she warned, and I feared she was right. Samuel wasn't all that keen about me to start with. Giving him more excuses to get rid of me was a bad idea for sure.

"I won't be gone long, Lois. I need to find June. It's important," I replied.

She paused for what seemed like a full minute before she said, "Whatever June needs, the hotel will provide. I told you that before. June is one of us."

I nodded, although she couldn't see me. "June needs a good lawyer, and it looks like she's got one. Pricey, too. Paige Weaver from Frontenac City. You know her?"

"Yes. We know her too well," Lois said without further explanation. "Take all the time you need, Andi, but you'd be wise to get back as soon as you can."

She hung up before I could say anything more. I looked at the phone as if it might speak on its own. I said, "Well, that was cryptic."

I snagged a golf cart outside the pro shop, and by nine o'clock, I was standing on June's doorstep, knocking. At first, I worried she wouldn't answer—I assumed she was home since her pink tricycle was parked out front—but then I heard the sound of a lock being turned, and she opened the door.

"Hey, June. We need to talk about Simon."

Her hand fluttered at her neck. "I'm not sure I know—"

"I talked to him last night. I know you two are engaged. Congratulations." I gestured to her left hand. "I saw your ring the other day before you tried to hide it with your gloves."

She opened the door, and I went inside.

"Is he here?" I asked, peeking into the kitchen.

"No. He didn't come back last night. I've been worried." Her hands were shaking. "You said you saw him?"

"Yeah, about nine. He told me about your engagement. He also confirmed that he'd seen Brittany in the maze shortly before she died."

She grabbed my arm. "He didn't kill her."

"Someone did. Do you know what she was involved in that might have induced someone to kill her?"

She frowned. "No, why would I? We aren't...weren't friends anymore. I didn't realize she was involved in anything like that. Something illegal?"

"Simon never mentioned anything about a guy named Tyler or Ackerman Biosystems?"

"No. Never." She shook her head.

"Have you talked to Tracy Hamlin recently?"

"Certainly not. That woman is horrid. I haven't talked to her since she came to my shop and called me a...a slut after she found out about Simon and me."

The conversation I'd had with Reggie and JC about June scratching up a car with gardening sheers over on the mainland popped into my head. I wondered whether that car had belonged to Tracy Hamlin. Before I could ask, there was a knock at the door.

I looked at June. "Are you expecting anyone?"

"No. I wasn't expecting you, either." She opened the door, and my stomach did a couple of flips and flops.

Sheriff Jackson stood on the stoop, along with two of his deputies. His eyes widened first, and then he scowled when he spotted me standing behind June.

"Hello, Sheriff," June said politely.

He held up a tri-folded paper. "June, I have a warrant to search your premises." He handed it to her. "If you will step outside while my deputies conduct the search, please."

She looked at me, and I grabbed hold of her arm and steered her outside. I took the warrant from her and looked it over. "It says they are authorized to search all the rooms in your house."

"What are they looking for?"

I glanced at the sheriff. "I think they're looking for plant seeds or leaves from plants like foxglove, oleander, and hemlock."

Her eyes widened. "Is that how Brittany died? She was poisoned?"

I nodded.

Once the deputies had their instructions, Sheriff Jackson stepped outside. "May I have a word with you?" He continued to walk down the lawn to the sidewalk.

I followed him.

"What are you doing here?" he asked.

"Consoling a friend," I said. "There's no law against that, is there?"

"Andi, I told you to stay out of this."

"No, actually you told me not to do anything dangerous." I put my hand on my hip as if I was making some kind of point. He kept looking steadily at me until I broke. "Okay. I came to talk to her about Simon Gervais."

He didn't even blink. It was like looking at solid granite. Mount Rushmore was softer than this guy.

I took a deep breath and told him the rest, all at once.

"Simon came to me. Last night. He said he'd seen Brittany in the maze that day. They'd arranged to meet there to talk about selling his part of the business to her. She got angry, threw the pink gloves at him—which were June's, by the way. He had bought them for her—and then he left."

He let out a long sigh and looked up at the sky. "This just gets better and better."

"They're engaged. June and Simon. That's why he wanted to divest himself of any interest in Brittany's business. I told Simon to call you, but before I could press the matter, he ran off like he was scared. I think possibly because he saw someone watching us."

He slow-blinked at me and shook his head.

Which was starting to piss me off. "You're looking at me like this is my fault. Simon called me, not the other way around. I didn't kill Brittany. I'm not secretly engaged to June. I'm not involved in something possibly illegal concerning plant DNA. I can't help it if people are…are weird."

"Weird?" His lips twitched upward.

"You're pressuring me," I huffed. "That was the first word that popped into my head."

He said, "I'm just standing here, doing my job."

"Which is the problem." I threw up my hands. "Your gaze is very intense. I imagine that's how you got elected, by glaring at everyone until they voted for you."

"Yes, that's exactly how it happened." He chuckled.

I inhaled deeply to calm my fluttering stomach. "June didn't kill Brittany. I'm sure of it."

One of the deputies stuck his head out of the door. "Sheriff. You need to come see this."

We made brief eye contact, and then the sheriff was striding up the lawn to the house. I followed in his wake. As he entered the house, June frowned at his retreating back and then looked toward me. "What's going on?"

I touched her shoulder on my way past. I followed him to the back of the house and into a workroom attached to the kitchen. There was a sturdy table lined up underneath a wide window. On top were several pots, bags of soil, plant food, a trowel, a few long sticks, plastic ties, and a black-and-white granite mortar and pestle. Next to the mortar was a foxglove plant, and its pretty purple flowers had missing petals. This was what everyone had gathered around.

The sheriff took out his phone and pulled up a photo. He lowered the phone next to the mortar, and then he nodded to the deputy. He gestured to the plants and all the tools on the table. "Bag and tag it. All of it."

When he turned and saw me, he glowered. "You can't be in here." He grabbed my arm and pulled me out of the room.

"What was in the mortar?"

"Crushed seeds."

"Foxglove seeds?" I asked, my guts churning.

"That's what it looks like. We'll have it tested to be sure."

We went out into the living room. "She might have crushed up the seeds, but June didn't have any opportunity to poison Brittany. They were not friendly. The only time they saw each other was at events like the Flower Festival. And that type of poison doesn't act that fast. It can take weeks, months even in low doses."

"June visited Brittany last month," he said.

My mouth fell open. "What? How do you know that?"

"A witness saw June in Brittany's house."

"Who's the witness?"

"Andi..."

"Just tell me." I knew he didn't have to tell me anything, but I hoped he would, knowing how important it was to me and to the Park.

"Tracy Hamlin."

I shook my head. "Tracy hates June. She'd say anything to get June in trouble."

"If that's true, I'll find out," he said, his voice softening a little. "But I have to follow the law and the evidence, Andi. Wherever it leads. You know that."

I nodded. "I know."

I went outside and stood beside June to support her through what was coming next.

The sheriff stepped outside the house. "June Biddle, I'm placing you under arrest for the murder of Brittany Gervais."

June gaped. "What? No. That's impossible... I didn't kill her." She looked at me, pleading. "Andi, help me."

I gave her shoulder a squeeze. "I will. Just go with Sheriff Jackson for now. We will get it all sorted out, I promise."

Tears rolled down her cheeks, and I had to swallow down my emotions, which were boiling to the surface. I wouldn't be any good to June or the Park if I lost my composure.

The sheriff took her arm and turned her so both her hands were behind her back. He placed handcuffs around her wrists. The final click of the metal lock sent a shiver down my back. As he read her Miranda rights, I walked beside June down to the sheriff's vehicle.

Neighbors had come out of their houses to watch. A car that had been driving by stopped in the middle of the street to gawk.

Rumors would be flying through the town within seconds, and there wasn't a damn thing I could do to stop them.

"I'll call Paige for you."

She nodded, her bottom lip quivering. "My birds?"

"I'll get Daisy to look after them, okay?"

"Okay."

The sheriff opened the back door and helped June into the seat. He shut the door and sighed. "You know I didn't want to do this."

"I know." I set my hand onto his bare forearm. He always had his shirt sleeves rolled up. "Will she be gone long?"

"Can't guarantee the judge will grant bail. She doesn't have a record and isn't a flight risk, so possibly. She won't see the judge till tomorrow, though."

"Okay. I'll call Paige and get the ball rolling."

He gave me a final sharp nod and then jumped into the vehicle. I watched him drive away as a lump formed in my throat. This was not how I expected any of this to go. June and Lois had asked for my help, and I felt like I'd failed them. I could only imagine how Samuel would take it all. And Ginny. She would be terribly upset because, well, that's how Ginny was. Softhearted and emotional about everyone she loved. And we all loved June.

CHAPTER TWENTY-ONE

SINCE I HAD TO talk to Daisy about taking care of June's birds, I stopped in at the pet hotel to enjoy some cat therapy before I returned to the Park to tell Lois the bad news. I needed to rub my face against Scout and Jem's fur and inhale their comforting kitty scent. Stroking them always made the three of us feel calmer.

When I walked into the kennel, Daisy looked up from feeding a carrot to a very hairy guinea pig and said, "You look like someone died. Again."

"The sheriff arrested June Biddle. I was there."

She stood. "Damn. That totally sucks."

"Yes, it totally does." I leaned on the counter. "Could you take care of her birds for a bit? She took them home a couple of days ago. I'll get you the house keys."

"Yeah, of course. I sold her those two kooky birds."

"Thanks. I know she'll appreciate it."

"We stick together, us villagers."

I nodded and pointed down the corridor to the pet hotel suites. "I'm just gonna…"

"Sure. They'll be so happy to see you."

When I opened the door to the suite and stepped inside, Scout had been lazing on the cat tree. Her eyes widened, and she sat up and meowed loudly. Jem, who had been inside one of the huts on the floor, crawled out and started to purr. I sat on the floor, and my two babies jumped onto my lap and rubbed against me.

For the next half hour, I was in perfect peace and harmony. The whole world fell away, and I didn't think about anything but how their purrs vibrated against my skin and the way their fur felt against my hands.

The moment I stepped into the Park Hotel and started to cross the lobby, every staff member's head turned my way. They had heard about June's arrest. Lois met me halfway, grabbed my arm, and herded me into her office.

"How bad is it?" she asked.

"There is evidence against her. It's mostly circumstantial. She had means and opportunity. And today, they found what they think was the murder weapon in her house. The arrest isn't airtight. But there's enough for a jury to convict her." I sat in one of the chairs. "I don't think they have a good motive, although they don't need one legally. But most juries won't convict for murder unless they feel the defendant had a strong motive."

Although…

The prosecution could probably paint a solid motive in June's relationship with Simon Gervais. Not because June had stolen her best friend's husband. But because Brittany couldn't buy him out, so he was still tied to her business, and it was failing fast. He'd be saddled with his share of the debt, and maybe Brittany's share, too, depending on the legal issues. Simon wanted to be completely free to marry June. If Brittany died, Simon would have been able to sell the business and maybe even make some money on the sale.

It was all too plausible.

Lois paced the room. "I can't believe it. June wouldn't hurt a fly."

I didn't say that everyone was capable of violence under the right conditions. Love, hate, jealousy, greed, revenge—these were powerful emotions and could be strong motives for murder.

"How can we help her?" Lois asked.

"I already called her lawyer."

Lois gave me a stern look. "You're a lawyer."

"I'm not licensed to practice in Michigan. And even in California, I wasn't a criminal defense attorney," I reminded her.

"I know," she sighed. "It's just I know you'd do your best. This other lawyer…"

"Paige Weaver." I figured she'd be dogged and fierce and competent, or Sheriff Jackson would never have recommended her to me. Or have dated her. "I'm sure she'll be a good lawyer for June."

"She'd better be, or I'll have something to say about it."

I grabbed Lois's hand. "It will be okay. June didn't kill Brittany. I feel as sure of that as you do. The truth will come out. It always does in the end."

I returned to my suite to do some more digging. I grabbed an apple from my refrigerator and settled down on the sofa with my laptop open and ready to go. First I searched *Tracy Hamlin Michigan*. A lot of pages came up with links for Tracy Hamlin the R&B singer. I scrolled over all of that. On the third page, I spotted a tiny mention of a student named Tracy Hamlin graduating from Michigan State University.

I clicked on the link. It took me to an alum page with pictures. I scrolled down and found Tracy's picture. She'd graduated with a degree in business. I kept scrolling through more pictures of other alumni. The pages were separated by the individual colleges and departments under the university umbrella. I took a chance and clicked on the College of Science alumni page and rolled past all the photos. I was just about to give up, when on the fourth page under the letter M, I found a picture of Tyler Montgomery.

So that was how they'd met. Tyler had been in college with Tracy, Brittany's sister. Which meant that was most likely how Tyler and Brittany knew each other, too. Now I just had to figure out what Tyler and Brittany were doing together all these years later.

Next I tried *Tyler Montgomery and Ackerman Biosystems*. Nothing came up linking them together. I scrolled through ten pages and found nothing helpful. I clicked on the images just to be thorough. I scrolled through a few staff photos. None featured Tyler. Then, way down on the page, I spotted a grainy picture inside a lab of some kind that must've been located in one of the Ackerman buildings. Taken three years ago, there were four people in lab coats doing science-like things. Two older men, a woman, and in the background scowling, looking like a creepy evil genius right out of central casting, was Tyler Montgomery.

So he had worked for Ackerman at one point, just as I'd suspected. Now that I'd made the connection, I wondered if he quit or got fired or whether he still worked there. And if any of that related to whatever he was working on with Brittany and why the two bioengineers were here at the hotel.

I took out my cell phone and punched in the number for Ackerman Biosystems. I got an automated answering system giving me a list of options that seemed to go on forever. I pressed nine for personnel and waited.

"Good afternoon, this is Fatima. How may I help you today?"

"Hello Fatima, this is"—my gaze landed on the floral arrangement on my table—"Rose calling from the Park, ah, Flower Company. I'm inquiring about one of your former employees, Tyler Montgomery. He's applied here for a position, and we need to confirm his dates of employment, etcetera."

"Tyler Montgomery?"

"Yes."

"Okay, please just give me a minute."

"Thank you." I could hear the click-clack of typing on a keyboard. Fatima must've had long nails.

After a few moments, she came back. "I'm sorry. We've never had an employee by that name working here."

"Are you sure? Would've been a couple of years back. He worked in one of the labs."

There was more typing and then a long pause. "I'm sorry. What did you say your name was again, and where are you calling from? I have a supervisor on hold for you."

I disconnected. Something was fishy there. Clearly, Tyler had worked there at one time—and maybe still did. I had photographic evidence staring me right in the face from my laptop screen. Had he been eliminated from the employee database? What on earth for? I wouldn't learn anything more on the phone.

An hour later, and the promise of a bottle of very expensive whisky to Nancy on the cleaning crew, I stood in the bioengineers' hotel suite. I brought some towels with me and two fuzzy bathrobes, which were stacked on the bed, in case they returned before I could do my search and get out.

I didn't know exactly what I was looking for, but that didn't stop me from opening every drawer in the dresser. There were no clothes there or anything else. They were only staying two days, so maybe not enough time to unpack, I guessed. I checked the closet for their suitcases. I found one, pulled it out, and plopped it onto the bed.

I unzipped it and quickly went through it, finding nothing of interest, except for a paperback book in German. I took it out and flipped through it. A business card fell out. I picked it up and saw it was for June's Blooms with the address of the shop and phone number. On the back was June's handwritten address.

I put the card back in the book and returned it to the suitcase. I then went through every pocket of every shirt and pair of pants in the case. In one pair of pants, I found another business card. Nature Path Pharmaceuticals with an address in Germany. I slipped the card into my pocket and then put the suitcase back where I'd found it.

I was closing the closet door when I heard the scraping of a key card at the door. Sometimes people didn't get the card into the slot properly on first try, lucky for me. I grabbed the towels and robes and went into the bathroom, carefully pulling the door almost, but not quite, closed.

I heard the door open and two sets of footsteps. The door closed with a snick, and two men continued speaking German. I had no idea what they were saying, but I did hear the name "Tyler" at least twice.

I slid my phone from my pocket and hit my voice recorder app. I held the phone toward the crack in the doorway, hoping I could catch some of the conversation. After another two minutes, I realized that I had to blow my cover or risk being discovered, which would have been beyond awkward. If I revealed myself now, they might believe I was in the room to deliver robes and towels.

I dropped my phone into my pocket and left it recording. I made noises as if I was organizing things and hummed a little tune while I worked. Then I opened the bathroom door and walked out into the room. I gasped, and my hand flew to my throat as I pretended to be startled by their presence.

"Oh my, I'm so sorry. I didn't realize you had returned to your room." I gave them a warm smile. I got two sets of frowns in return.

"What are you doing here?" Trent asked.

"I'm Andi Steele, the concierge. We met the other day?"

No response. *Wow, tough crowd.*

"I'm helping out with room service today. We're short-handed. I was stocking your bathroom with fresh towels and clean robes. I hope you try them. They are so luxurious, just like a spa robe."

They glanced at each other, probably trying to decide how much of my palaver they were going to swallow.

I kept up the running chatter on my way to the exit. "Speaking of the spa. Have you tried the massages there?"

Keith shook his head.

"So amazing. Tell you what, why don't I hook you two up with a free thirty-minute massage?" I pulled out another business card from my pants pocket—thank goodness I always kept a stack of them on hand—and grabbed the pen from the desk nearby. I wrote down FREE MASSAGE on the back. I handed the card to the closest one. "Just take this to Carmen at the spa, and she will set you up."

"Thank you," Keith said, his German accent noticeably absent. He sounded like a regular American from Michigan again.

"I'll just get out of your hair." I walked to the door and opened it. "You gentlemen have a great day."

I walked quickly down the corridor to the stairs and down to the lobby. I pulled out my phone and held it to my ear to listen to the recording. I turned up the volume. The sound was weak, but I could definitely hear German conversation in my ear. I had no idea what they'd been saying, but I knew the perfect person to translate for me. And while I was there, I'd get my favorite apple strudel.

Chapter Twenty-two

THERE WERE ONLY A few customers enjoying the pastry at the Weiss Strudel House when I arrived. Lena Weiss waved at me when I came in, as she always did.

"Hello, hello, Andi." Her voice was heavily accented and as delightful as her strudel. She came around the counter to give me a hug, shuffling her feet on the tiled floor.

I hugged her, inhaling the scent of freshly baked bread and cinnamon she always carried with her. "How are you today, Mrs. Weiss?"

"Not too bad, dear. But my knees hurt, so I think it's going to rain."

I looked out the window at the bright sun in the blue sky. "It might. You never know."

"I will get you your usual." She shuffled behind the counter and opened the back of the display case to pluck out one fat delicious-looking apple strudel. "Any cherry for the boys?"

"No, not today."

I usually bought cherry strudel for Reggie and JC down at the docks. I traded the pastries for information, but it was not their information I was in need of today.

Lena placed the pastry carefully into a little white paper bag and sat it on the counter for me. "Anything else, dear?"

"How's your hearing?"

Ten minutes later, I was in the kitchen with Lena and Wilhelm, holding out my phone so they could listen to the German language recording. I pushed play. The voices were faint and a bit tinny.

"Give to me. I listen." Frowning, Wilhelm took the phone from my hand. He held it up to his ear.

"One says, 'We have been looking for Tyler for over twenty-four hours. Maybe we won't find him.' The other says, 'He's here somewhere. He got to the greenhouse before we could. Also that annoying woman from the hotel is interfering with our business.'"

Oh, I didn't like the sound of that. I was the annoying woman from the hotel. And he'd called me that even before he knew I'd snuck into their room. Which meant my actions had been justified, once again.

"The other then says, 'We paid him and Brittany for the product. We have to find it and deliver it.' Then the other says, 'We need the formulas as well. Matthias will pay us double to recover that from Ackerman.'" Wilhelm handed the phone back to me. "The rest is you sweet-talking them."

Taking the phone, I smiled. "Thank you so much. You've been a huge help."

I left the bakery and sat in the golf cart for a moment while I used the search engine on my phone. I looked up Nature Path Pharmaceuticals, the name on the business card I'd taken from the hotel room suitcase. Nature Path was based in Munich, Germany, and specialized in naturopathic medicines. I flipped through pages of the website and found the page listing the board of directors. One of them was Matthias Richter, the guy those two guys were talking about when I taped their conversation.

Time to take this info to the sheriff.

Fortunately, Deputy Shawn was not manning the front when I came in. It was the pleasant Deputy Marshall with the cherub cheeks and big brown eyes.

"Good afternoon, Miss Steele. What can I do for you?"

"Is the sheriff in?"

"Yes, he is."

He buzzed me through the half door, and I approached the sheriff's office. The door was closed, but I did a quick, brisk knock, opened it, and walked in. I expected Sheriff Jackson to give me a frowny look and bark something stern. What I didn't expect was Paige Weaver sitting on the edge of his desk, her long, thin legs clad in sheer hose under a form-fitting pencil skirt that every woman on earth would covet, laughing at something he'd just said.

I froze. "Ah, I'm sorry to intrude."

The sheriff rose to his feet, clearing his throat. "You're not intruding on anything."

"We were just talking about old times," Paige said as she dangled one shapely leg that suggested she worked out about two hours a day. I hadn't worked out in…well, a long time.

"Should I come back?" I asked pointedly to the sheriff.

"No." He gestured to the chair. "Now is good."

Paige got off the desk and took the chair closest to the desk. I went around her and sat in the other chair. Sheriff Jackson re-seated himself in his desk chair, seemingly oblivious to the posturing occurring in front of him.

"What can I help you with, Andi?" he asked.

"How is June?"

"My client," Paige piped up before the sheriff could, "is resting comfortably, considering the circumstances."

"I have some evidence that I think will help to exonerate June."

Paige's eyes widened. "I've heard you were tenacious, but I had no idea."

I ignored her, although I did want to know who she'd heard that from. My bet was on Sheriff Jackson, who was squirming in his chair. I could tell he was slightly uncomfortable. Served him right.

I gave them the rundown of what I'd learned about Tyler, Ackerman Biosystems, and the two Germans who were guests at the hotel pretending to be on vacation. Sheriff Jackson scribbled in his notebook as I talked. I played the recorded conversation from my phone and paraphrased what Wilhelm had translated.

"So, you're thinking corporate espionage?" the sheriff asked.

I nodded. "Tyler once worked at Ackerman. I figure he stole proprietary research, maybe some formulas, and struck a deal with a German company to sell the info for new drugs."

"Created from common flowers and plants known to be poisonous for decades?" Paige said with a skeptical look on her face. "How much money would anyone pay for that?"

"There are a lot of natural uses that can be derived from hemlock, and oleander and foxglove. More and more people are turning to natural remedies to treat all kinds of ailments." I thought about Ginny's consistent use of essential oils and vitamins to treat everything from blemishes to toe fungus to the flu. Naturopathic treatments were a billion-dollar industry. "Digoxin is a drug used by heart specialists for some heart conditions. It comes from the seeds of the foxglove plant. I suspect it's what you found in the mortar in June's house."

The sheriff frowned as he slid a file from the side of his desk and opened it. His finger traced over some form.

"A massive dose of digoxin was found in Brittany's system on the preliminary toxicology screen. Dose strong enough to kill her," he said, still running his finger down the list. "Several other substances that the doc couldn't identify yet, too."

I winced. The evidence pointed so clearly to June. She simply couldn't have killed Brittany. I didn't believe it. I refused to believe it.

"Do you think the digoxin we found in June's house was planted there by these German bioengineers?" the sheriff asked.

"They had her address, so it's possible," I said. "What does June say about it?"

"She said she'd never grind up foxglove seeds in her workroom like that. That digoxin is too dangerous to mess around with, without the proper equipment and ventilation," Paige Weaver replied. "With long-term exposure, poisonous plants can be fatal. Mixing toxic plants together would be lunacy. June is too smart for that."

I nodded. For once, the dragon lady and I were in full agreement. "I think Tyler and Brittany met through Tracy Hamlin, and together, Tyler and Brittany had been fiddling around with different plant species to make generic naturopathic drugs to sell to Nature Path Pharmaceuticals. Remember that both Tyler and Brittany had similar rashes on their hands. And I'm reasonably sure it was Tyler I caught stealing something from inside the greenhouse. They might have stored samples there, in addition to the paperwork for their formulas."

"These two bioengineers arrived on the island after Brittany died." Sheriff Jackson drummed his fingers on his desk. "Is there another player we're missing?"

"Simon Gervais," Paige and I said at the same time. She glared at me, and I glared right back.

"Simon knew Brittany's business was in trouble. She was on the verge of bankruptcy, which would probably have put a serious dent in Simon's lifestyle, too," I said. "He had to have known Brittany was trying to save the business. Maybe she told him outright, got him involved." My heartbeat picked up, and I leaned forward in the chair. I was definitely onto something. I could feel it. "When I saw Simon last night, he got spooked and ran. Someone had been watching us from the trees. I found a cigarette butt, still smoldering. And it had a strange odor to it. Not like American tobacco."

"The Germans?" Sheriff Jackson asked.

"Could be." I nodded, but I hadn't found similar cigarettes or any of the usual smoker paraphernalia like lighters or matches in their room. And neither of them had smelled like smoke when they walked into their room or the time I'd talked to them in the café. I had a sensitive nose to these things.

The sheriff leaned back in his chair and rubbed a hand through his hair. The stubble on his chin was dark, but I noticed a little gray peppered in there. He looked tired.

Like me, I imagined he hadn't been sleeping well because of this case. It had to be hard on him to see June in a jail cell. He liked June as much as the rest of us did. He wouldn't be happy to see her convicted. Just the opposite. He was dedicated to serving the village and the people in it.

"I'll put a call in to Frank Nelson over in Frontenac City. Ask him to bring Tyler and Tracy in for questioning," he said, as if he was making his own list of things to do in his head.

"What about the Germans?" I asked.

"I'll go have a talk with them. What room are they in?"

"Room 312."

Paige patted me awkwardly on the shoulder. "Well done, Andi. You made my job easy."

"Well, whatever you may have heard from the gossip mill, I'm still a damn good lawyer."

"I never put any stock in gossip," she said, her eyes wide in mock surprise.

"Uh-huh." I stood. "Can I see June?"

The sheriff's "Of course" battled with Paige's "No" in the room.

He stood and came around the desk. "I'll take you."

"Luke…" Paige warned.

"This is my station, Paige. My rules."

She huffed but didn't argue with him. She remained seated as the sheriff and I moved toward the door. He stopped and glanced at her. "You'll have to wait out in the lobby."

With one sharply defined eyebrow arched, she grabbed her purse from his desk and walked out of the office. A trail of expensive rose-scented perfume wafted behind her. I wrinkled my nose. I didn't know what brand of perfume she was wearing, but it didn't work on her at all.

I followed the sheriff down the back corridor of the station to the cells. There were two of them. One was larger, an open area with several benches and metal bars. This was typically the "drunk tank." The other cell was a small room with a glass pane in the steel door. Inside was a bed, toilet, sink, and one steel guest chair. It was spartan but clean enough. There was a window over the bed to let in the natural light.

June was resting on the narrow bed when the sheriff unlocked the door. She sat up and smiled when she saw me. I went in and sat on the chair beside her bed. The sheriff closed the door on his way out, but he didn't lock it. He'd probably be waiting just outside.

"Are they letting me go?" she asked. The eagerness in her voice stabbed me in the stomach.

"Soon, I hope." I didn't want to give her false expectations. I was positive that the information I'd given the sheriff, along with the follow-up he'd undertake, would exonerate June. But stuff like that could take time. Probably a few days at least, and maybe more, to sort it all out and get the judge to drop all charges and release her from custody.

There was just one more piece of the puzzle that needed to be found and placed into position.

"June, you knew what Brittany and Tyler were doing with the drug formulas, didn't you?"

She nodded.

"How about Simon? Did he know?"

Her gaze dropped to the floor, and I thought maybe she was going to tell me some story. "I think so. He mentioned that soon Brittany would be able to buy him out. He said she'd promised to pay twice what he was owed if he could wait a little longer. He promised that once he had the money, we would run away to the Bahamas and get married on the beach."

I nodded. "Did Simon ever mention exactly what they were producing? Any specifics?"

"He asked me a lot of questions about plant-based drugs, what could produce what. So, I assumed they were playing around with the genetics of several plants to produce different compounds. At first, I thought they were just growing medical-grade marijuana. There's a lot of money to be made there. But after I overheard a few phone calls, I knew it was more serious."

"Phone calls from who?"

She shrugged. "I'm not sure, but Simon started to get paranoid. He said people would come for him."

"What people?"

"I don't know. I figured he was just being silly. Anxious about what Brittany and Tyler were doing."

I put my hand on top of hers and gave her a reassuring squeeze. "Do you know where Simon is?"

She sighed. "He has a boat at the marina. He's been staying there when he hasn't been at my place."

"Thanks, June. You're doing the right thing. Hang in there." I gave her clasped hands a little squeeze and stood. I knocked lightly, and Sheriff Jackson opened the door for me.

Before I walked out, June asked, her voice low and small, "He set me up, didn't he? Simon. He put those ground seeds in my workroom, knowing the sheriff would find them."

I didn't say anything. I had no idea how to comfort her after a massive betrayal like that. I was still trying to soothe my own heart and soul from the wounds I'd suffered with Jeremy's betrayal, and I'd never given him my heart. Not like June had given hers to Simon.

I left the cell, and the sheriff closed and locked the door behind me.

"Simon's got a boat docked at the marina," I said to him.

CHAPTER TWENTY-THREE

WHILE THE SHERIFF MADE calls over to the mainland and Paige was on the phone to the judge, I headed back to the hotel. I had news to deliver to Lois, and I needed to actually sit down and eat something. I'd been on the go for the past six hours without so much as a pee break.

As I crossed the lobby, I waved to Lane, who was covering the concierge desk. He was in his glory, beaming at the guest he was talking to. I suspected I was going to really have to keep my eyes open. He had ambition written all over him. Ambition wasn't necessarily a bad thing, but I didn't need him aimed at usurping me. Not when I still had Casey Cushing to deal with, too.

I was about to knock at Lois's office door, but I heard voices inside and lowered my arm. This time, she wasn't talking to Henry the imaginary ghost. That would have been easier to handle. Instead, Lois and Samuel were having a lively debate. About me.

Lois said heatedly, "Andi is an asset to this hotel. She is friendly, efficient, organized, and goes above and beyond the call of duty. She cares about this hotel and especially the people who run it. Besides, you're open to the idea of having two concierges, not one. Problem solved."

"That may be, Lois. But Casey has seniority here. He's been with us for years. Loyalty counts for something with me. We planned to hold his job for him. We owe him his job back once he returns from his extended personal leave. I don't expect this two-concierge thing Andi came up with to work. And when it fails, we'll be back to Casey. Simple as that," Samuel replied with as much gusto.

"We're not contractually obligated to give Casey the concierge job when he returns. We said we'd have a job waiting for him. And if having two concierges doesn't pan out, we will find a place for him. Somewhere in the company," Lois insisted.

"Be reasonable. We gave him our word. Our word means something here at the Park, Lois," Samuel said sternly, like his was the only word that mattered.

Which was when Lois played the trump card. "Henry agrees with me about Andi. He likes her. He's always liked her. And you damn well know Henry never liked Casey Cushing one whit."

I could hear Samuel's huge exhalation of breath. I could just imagine the withering look he gave his daughter-in-law for thinking she could still rely on his dead son to win any kind of argument.

"Lois…" he warned.

"I know. I know." I imagined her putting her hand up, palm out toward him in the universal gesture to stop. I'd seen her do it during countless conversations when she simply didn't want to hear. "Henry is dead. Don't think I don't know that, Sam. I do. Every blasted day, I know it, feel it. But it helps me to talk to him. It helps to know he hears and replies to me, too, even if he doesn't communicate with you. And I know, without a shadow of a doubt, he'd want Andi here. She was like a second daughter to him."

Tears pricked at my eyes, and a lump formed in my throat. I had fallen in love with Ginny's family years ago. From the moment I'd met them during our first year of college. They had taken me in so easily when they knew that my parents were absent in all kinds of ways. Every Thanksgiving and Christmas, I'd spent with the Park family. Henry had been so full of life and joy. I could still hear his rumbling chuckles echoed in his son's laughter. And Henry had laughed a lot. Missing his funeral was one of my biggest regrets. But like Lois, I remembered Henry when he was vibrant and so alive. He was impossible to forget, even if we wanted to. Which we didn't.

If Lois wanted to pretend Henry was still alive, she was hurting no one. Even if she thought his ghost was still here, so what? There was no reason not to indulge her. Her behavior didn't necessarily mean she'd lost her grip or anything.

As I stood there contemplating whether to knock or to leave and come back later, a puff of warm air brushed against my face. The scents of vanilla, cinnamon, and orange filled my nose. I looked around me to see if someone had passed by, but I was alone in the corridor. The smell came again, stronger, as if someone wearing Old Spice aftershave had enveloped me in a warm hug.

Henry was the only man I'd ever known who wore Old Spice. I remembered burying my nose in his sweater every time he gave me a welcome or goodbye hug, simply because the smell was singularly his.

"Henry?" I whispered.

Suddenly, the door to the office opened, and Samuel looked out. "Andi. How long have you been standing there?"

I shook my head free of the memories. "Just got here and was about to knock."

He eyed me, knowing full well I'd been standing outside the door the entire time. "I've made a decision about your job."

"Great." I gave him a tight smile.

"As you know, when Casey returns, you will both be involved in the concierge duties."

I opened my mouth, but he glared me into closing it quick.

"I've talked to a few bigger hotels. Other duties will be incorporated into the job description. Ginny has been asking for some help with event planning, so when one of you isn't on the desk, you will be assisting Ginny with whatever needs done."

"Sounds fair."

He gave a sharp nod. "Good. So, we'll hear no more of it." He patted my shoulder. "I may not have my son's affable disposition, but I know a good worker when I see one."

"Thank you, Samuel."

He dropped his hand and marched away. Since I'd overheard the whole conversation he'd just had with Lois, I knew this wasn't the end of the discussion. But my situation had advanced. Now, if the two-concierge thing didn't work out, at least Lois would be on my side.

I went into the office and closed the door behind me. Lois sat at her desk with her head in her hands. "Arguing with Samuel is like wrestling with an alligator, Henry always said."

"You are the finest alligator wrestler I've ever met." I sat in the soft leather chair.

She steepled her fingers and gave me a weary smile. "Please give me some good news."

I smiled. "Happy to oblige. I'm pretty sure June will be out of jail soon and the charges against her dropped."

"That's great news." She slapped her hand down on the desk. "I knew you'd fix it."

"Well, there are some things the sheriff needs to take care of, and it's not a done deal yet. But I suspect by this time next week, June will be back to making her beautiful floral arrangements for the Park Hotel."

"Fantastic. Like I told Samuel, you're a real asset to the Park, Andi." She paused. "We're lucky to have you."

"Thank you, Lois. That means a lot to me." I stood, eager to return to my suite and maybe have a little nap. Before I left, though, I turned to her. "I wanted to tell you that I regret not coming to Henry's funeral. I'm sorry I wasn't there. To be with you. To support you."

Lois got up and came around the desk. She hugged me. "Everyone understood why you couldn't make it, Andi. Please don't feel guilty." She patted me on the back. "Henry knows you care about him."

That warm air and Old Spice scent enveloped me again, and I accepted that it was Henry forgiving me. Why not? Lots of old buildings had ghosts. Merely enhanced the reputation and appeal of the hotel. It might even become a tourist attraction—who knew? I left Lois's office feeling a bit lighter than I'd felt before. Lighter than I'd felt since arriving at the Park, honestly.

When I returned to my suite, I immediately collapsed on my bed and fell asleep. I'd intended to only nap for an hour, but three hours later, I finally blinked open my eyes and rolled off the bed. My stomach growled its annoyance at having been neglected for so long.

It was such beautiful evening, I decided to treat myself and order in room service and eat out on my patio. When my food arrived, I took it out to the patio table, sat, and savored every morsel of the grilled steak and lobster with asparagus and salad. A nice red wine complemented everything perfectly for my taste.

My cell phone buzzed at me, and I checked to see several texts from Daniel. He'd called and left a message this morning. I had expected annoyance over my antics at Brittany's greenhouse, but he didn't sound angry, just maybe a bit disappointed and possibly fed up. I was being a coward by not returning his call, but I knew what I had to do, and I simply didn't want to do it yet.

Daniel's texts made it clear I might not have to do anything at all.

I want to make sure you're okay.

I heard about the break-in.

This isn't working between us, is it?

And there it was. The toughest question. The one I'd been ignoring because I didn't want to answer it.

After I put the last bit of lobster in my mouth, chewed, and swallowed, I picked up my phone and dialed Daniel. It was time to be a grownup about this and stop dangling the carrot in front of him. The stick was quicker, and the sharp thwap of it would be over in minutes. My answer would sting for a bit, but the sting would fade. A man like Daniel already had a long, long line of women waiting for the chance to treat him like he deserved.

"Hey, you," he answered on the second ring.

"I'm sorry I didn't call earlier."

"It's okay. I imagine you've been busy."

"Yeah." I scraped the fork across the plate to distract me from what I had to do. "So, I was thinking…"

"That doesn't sound promising."

That made me chuckle, and I lifted my head. Out of the corner of my eye, I spotted fast movement not far from my patio on the pathway along the bluff. Squinting into the dark, I made out a male quick-walking, every now and then glancing back over his shoulder. As he passed under the lamp, I saw that it was Tyler.

"Andi?"

"Oh, sorry…"

Behind Tyler, coming at a fast clip, were the two German bioengineers. This was not a moonlight stroll by either party.

"Oh crap. I'm sorry, Daniel. I've got to go." I disconnected and slid my phone into my pants pocket as I was getting to my feet. I jumped up onto the partition separating my patio from the grassy knoll and ran out onto the path.

I jogged along the main pathway, looking left and right toward several trails that branched off. The sun had fully set, the twilight ended. The spattering of lamps here and there gave off pools of light, but if the men had veered off into the grass or behind some bushes, I wouldn't be able to see them.

I should've called the sheriff, but it would take him time to get here. Time I didn't think Tyler had. I was unarmed. I didn't even have my purse, so no pepper spray. But I had my wits and determination. Hopefully, that would be enough. Although neither wits nor determination would stop a bullet, if they had guns.

To the right, I spotted three dark forms. One of the shadows was on the ground, the other two loomed over. I bolted toward them. Tyler was the one on the ground. Trent was leaning over him, his hand going into his coat pocket.

"Stop! Don't hurt him!"

Trent and Keith twisted toward me as I charged forward, my arms extended. I pushed Keith hard, and he stumbled to the side.

"Hey! Why did you do that?"

"You were going to kill him."

Trent frowned. "Don't be ridiculous. I'm calling an ambulance. Tyler doesn't look good." In Trent's hand was a phone, not a gun. He made the call to 9-1-1.

I crouched down by Tyler and saw that he was curled into the fetal positon. His skin was slick with sweat, and he'd vomited. I touched his forehead. He was feverish. He'd been poisoned.

"Tyler? Can you hear me?"

He mumbled something and then rocked back and forth.

I looked up at Trent and Keith. "What happened?"

"We met up, and then he just freaked out and ran," Trent said. "When we caught up to him, he collapsed onto the ground."

I grabbed Tyler's wrist and pressed my fingers to it. His heartbeat was irregular. I suspected he would soon have died, just like Brittany.

"Have you seen his symptoms before?" I asked.

Trent nodded. "He's having a toxic reaction to a substance."

"Foxglove?"

"Yes, but I've never seen a reaction like this. It's like foxglove poisoning, and oleander poisoning, and hemlock poisoning all rolled into one. This is too fast for just one poison."

I heard the wail of the ambulance and saw the approach of the whirling lights. I stood and waved my hands. "Here! Over here!"

Trent and Keith took up my cry, waving their arms around, and I saw two EMTs running toward us. Behind them, I spotted

Sheriff Jackson fast on their heels. My heart swelled at the sight of him.

While the paramedics worked on Tyler, the sheriff grabbed my arm. "Are you okay?"

"Yes, I'm not hurt."

He glanced at the Germans, his hand going to his weapon.

I put my hand on his. "You don't need it. They weren't trying to hurt Tyler. They just wanted to talk to him."

The paramedics got Tyler on a stretcher and carried him back to the ambulance.

Trent watched them go, then nodded. "We've been trying to connect with Tyler for weeks. He'd stopped returning our calls. We got worried."

"You work for Nature Path Pharmaceuticals," Sheriff Jackson said.

"Yes, I do." Keith took out his wallet and handed the sheriff a business card.

"And I work for Ackerman Biosystems," Trent said as he fished out the ID card I'd seen in his wallet.

"Tyler didn't steal proprietary research from Ackerman?" I asked, wondering how I'd got it wrong.

"No, of course not."

I frowned. "I called, and the woman I talked to said that Tyler Montgomery never worked there."

Trent made a face. "That's because he never did work for us."

"I saw a picture of him in a lab at Ackerman," I said.

Trent nodded. "I remember that day. He was a guest, on loan from Nature Path."

"Tyler works for Nature Path?" the sheriff asked.

Trent nodded. "We were in business with Tyler and Brittany. They were making a new drug for us by crossbreeding a couple of toxic flowers. The drug would be revolutionary."

It all sounded too perfect, too above board. And if it truly was, then why…

I said, "If Tyler was working for both companies, why wasn't he working in a structured, bonafide lab with rigid safety protocols if the drug was going to be so revolutionary?"

Trent looked at Keith, who dropped his gaze. Bingo.

"He wasn't working for either company," the sheriff said. "This whole operation was off the books, which is why Tyler was using a backyard greenhouse for his lab."

These men may not have murdered Brittany or tried to murder Tyler, but they definitely shared responsibility.

"I'm going to need the both of you to come down to the station to formalize this conversation." The sheriff tapped his fingers against his belt, where his sidearm was holstered.

Trent put his cell phone to his ear. "I'm calling our lawyer."

Sheriff Jackson nodded. "That's probably a good idea." He gestured for the men to walk toward the main lobby of the hotel where his vehicle was parked. Then he glanced at me. "Do you want me to drop you off at the hospital, or do you want to come to the station to help sort this all out?"

I loved that he didn't offer to escort me back to my suite or tuck me somewhere safe and sound and far from the action. He knew me well enough to know that such a move wouldn't stick and I'd be back right in the middle of things.

"Actually I'm going home. I think I may have left my balcony door wide open."

His eyebrows lifted in surprise, and it nearly made me chuckle. "I'll talk to you later, then."

I nodded. "Most likely."

He started to walk toward the lobby while I went across the park to my suite. I stopped and called to him, "Hey, make sure you ask the doc to test Tyler's bloodwork against Brittany's. It would make sense that they both suffered from the same poisoning."

He flipped his hand in a backward wave to signal that he'd heard me and continued on his way. I saw the slight shake of his head, and it made me smile.

As I approached my patio, I saw that, yes, I had left my patio door open in my haste to spring into action. Closer to the partition, I caught a whiff of sweet cigarette smoke and wondered who'd been smoking nearby. I'd get someone in the grounds department to fix that. We needed a sign that said *No Smoking Near the Hotel* or something like that.

When I jumped over the partition and back onto my patio, instantly I realized something was wrong. My whole body started to shake as I stepped into my suite through the gaping glass door. Swallowing down the bile rising in my throat, I took in the destruction before me.

My entire suite had been trashed.

The cushions on the sofa had been slashed open, and the stuffing was strewn all over the carpet. Every shelf in the living room had been cleared, the books open on the floor, the knickknacks broken, pieces scattered about. Careful not to step on things, I saw that every drawer in my small kitchen was open, and the contents tossed on the floor. I was shaking by the time I reached my bedroom.

The covers had been stripped from the bed, and the pillows slashed. All my dresser drawers were open, panties and bras sticking out, and a few tossed about. My closet had been riffled through. Pants were thrown on the bed, the pocket linings protruding as if they'd been turned inside out. The only thing intact was my giant unicorn.

I rushed back to the living room, pushing cushion stuffing off the table. My laptop was gone. All the blood drained from my head, and I felt faint. Slowly, I lowered myself to the floor, putting my head between my legs to breathe.

CHAPTER TWENTY-FOUR

GINNY PLACED A CUP of hot tea into my cold hands as we sat out on the patio while two deputies picked through the wreckage in my suite, taking pictures and making lists of the things that had been destroyed.

After nearly hyperventilating because my place had been wrecked, I'd called 9-1-1. I hadn't expected the sheriff to come because I knew he was busy, but I had secretly wished he'd put everything else aside and come running. It was a foolish notion, and I had no business thinking about it.

"Are you sure you don't want to come back to my place? I could run you a hot bath so you could warm up," Ginny said. "You're still shaking."

"I'm okay."

"Andi, there is nothing okay with this."

"I know. I'm trying not to think about that."

She rubbed a hand over my back. "I can't believe someone would just come and wreck your stuff. Makes no sense. You don't think it was that Clive Barrington, do you?"

"What?"

"Clive Barrington. The hottie from Hong Kong you were trying to set me up with. Amazing eyes, by the way. Never seen anything like that before." She paused to widen her eyes and shake her hand as if she'd grabbed something too hot to handle. "Didn't I tell you we had coffee? All he did was ask questions about you the whole time. He seemed really smitten with you. What the heck did you say to the guy at that concierge desk, anyway?"

"What kind of questions was he asking?"

"Were you dating anyone, what was your job here, how long were you planning to stay," Ginny rattled off. "Like that. Things a guy would ask if he was interested in you."

I was already upset about my suite, and now some guy just happened to show up here—from Hong Kong, no less—asking my best friend questions about me. It was too much to think about. And Ginny was right. It didn't make any sense that someone would want to destroy my suite.

Because that's not what had happened. This wasn't senseless destruction. This was both a search for something and a message. I had no idea who would do this, what they were looking for, or why. But this was most definitely deliberate.

Deputy Marshall took one last photo then stepped out onto the patio. "I should take your statement now, Miss Steele."

I nodded, while he looked at his clipboard and wrote down some info on the witness statement form.

"I'll do it, Marshall." I looked up to see the sheriff come up behind the deputy and take the clipboard from him. A surge of relief flowed through me, and I sagged against the chair. He nodded toward his deputy. "You finish up inside."

"Okay, Sheriff." Deputy Marshall stepped back into my suite.

Sheriff Jackson looked me over, his brow furrowed into worry lines. "Are you sure you want to do this here?"

I nodded.

Ginny's cell phone buzzed. "It's Mom." She answered.

While Ginny stepped away to talk to Lois, the sheriff sat in one of the chairs near me, his knee touching mine. It was such a simple thing, almost innocuous, but it felt right. Comforting. Supportive. I wasn't even sure he consciously knew what he'd done.

"Take your time telling me."

"After we parted on the path, I walked across the lawn to my suite. I knew I had stupidly left the balcony door open."

"Open or just unlocked?"

"Open, wide open. When I approached, I saw that something was wrong inside. I could see some of the destruction when I reached the glass door. I stepped inside and saw everything ruined."

"Did you have to push the door open or could you just walk in?

"Just walked in."

"Did you notice anything odd before you entered the suite? Any movement nearby? Any voices? Any—"

"I smelled cigarette smoke right here at the partition." I gestured to the cement berm behind me.

"And you don't smoke."

"No."

He got up and went over to the partition. He looked over it, to the left and to the right near some bushes. He reached down and plucked something from the ground. He brought it over to me. It was a cigarette butt with a gray filter.

"Marshall," he called into the suite, "bring me an evidence bag."

The deputy, seeing what was in his hand, opened up a small evidence bag, and the sheriff dropped the butt inside. Marshall sealed it and wrote on it, and then he put it into his pocket.

The sheriff pointed to the bushes behind the partition. "Take a couple of photos there."

The deputy did as asked and then went back inside.

"How long were you gone? From leaving to find Tyler to returning home?"

"An hour at most."

He sat down, his knee touching mine again. "Did you notice anything out of the ordinary before you went chasing after Tyler?"

"You think whoever did this was waiting nearby?"

"Doesn't seem random. It seems like a perfect opportunity taken by someone who was looking for one."

I thought about the cigarette butt I had found in the trees when Simon and I had been talking. At the time, it seemed logical that it was someone watching Simon, the Germans even, but now...now whoever it was might have been watching me. But who and why?

The only person that popped into my mind was Jeremy Rucker.

He'd called me, sent me flowers, and had left a fairly ominous note: *See you soon.* But why would he do this? I just couldn't see it. He'd have no reason to scare me like this. We'd been colleagues for years, friends even, and whoever had done this was looking for something specific. I'd practically been marched out of our firm's offices with a single box filled with the totality of my meager belongings. I had nothing Jeremy could possibly want.

Sheriff Jackson nudged my knee. "What are you thinking? I can tell you're running through scenarios in your head."

"Jeremy."

"Who's that? Ex-boyfriend?"

"Not at all. Jeremy Rucker was my boss back in California. He was arrested for embezzlement."

His eyes narrowed. "And why did you make that connection?"

"He's been sending me flowers, and he called me once when I first moved here."

"What does he want?"

I shrugged. "Nothing, as far as I can tell. To apologize, to see how I am doing."

"You were never romantically involved?" he asked.

"Certainly not. Besides, he was married."

"And you weren't the one who had him arrested?

I shook my head. "I hadn't even known it happened. I went to work one morning, and the partners gave me the heave-ho and sent me on my way."

He made some notes on the form. "Was anything taken tonight?"

"My laptop."

He grimaced at that. "That sucks."

"It certainly does."

He made more notes and then looked at me. "Do you have somewhere to sleep?"

For some reason, the blue sofa in his house popped into my mind. I could easily see myself comfortably sleeping on it.

I began to open my mouth, but Ginny jumped in, putting her arm around my shoulders. "She's staying with me. And I just talked to Lois, and we'll get you a new suite to move into tomorrow."

"That's good," Sheriff Jackson said.

"Is it okay that I go in and get some of Andi's things?" Ginny asked. "I don't think she should have to do that."

He nodded. "Just let Marshall know what you're doing."

Ginny squeezed my shoulder. "I'll be right back."

I closed my eyes briefly and took in a deep breath of fresh air. When I opened my eyes again, the sheriff had taken my hand, which had been shaking in my lap. His skin was warm against mine.

"I'll find out who did this, Andi. I promise."

I gave him a small smile. "I know."

He returned it. "That's high praise considering when I first met you, you thought I was an incompetent rube."

"I wouldn't have said rube…"

He chuckled, and I suddenly wanted him to wrap his arms around me and hold me tight. I knew, if he did, that nothing could harm me, nothing could make me feel alone and sad ever again. Licking my lips, I leaned forward in the chair, toward him. I knew it was the most horrible, most inconvenient, most inappropriate time, but I wanted to kiss Sheriff Jackson. I think maybe I'd wanted to from the moment I met him, even if the kiss would only wipe that stern scowl from his lips.

His eyes widened, and I could hear his breath intake in surprise, but he didn't pull back. His thumb rubbed slowly over the knuckles of my hand. The heat from his touch was rising up my arm, filling me with a fever that I hadn't felt in a very long time.

I wasn't positive this was the right thing to happen between us. It would definitely change our relationship, our dynamic. Right at this moment, though, I didn't care. All I wanted was to feel Luke's lips on mine, to feel his want for me. And for the first time, I realized, I'd just thought of him as Luke, not just Sheriff Jackson or the sheriff.

"I wasn't sure what to grab." Ginny walked out onto the patio, her head down looking through the bag she'd filled with some of my things. She looked up at us.

Luke pulled his hand away and leaned back in the chair. I wasn't quick enough and was still leaning forward.

Ginny's eyes widened, and she made an O with her mouth. "Whoops. Do I have bad timing or what?"

I shook my head. "You're fine. The sheriff and I were just finishing up with my statement." I reached for the clipboard. "Should I just sign the bottom?"

He nodded.

I did and handed the board back to him.

"Thanks. I'll keep you posted. I'll put out the word to the pawn shops on the mainland to see if your laptop turns up."

"I have a feeling that's not going to happen."

I didn't think petty thieves looking for fast cash had broken into my place. Whoever did it would break into my laptop and then dispose of it. I had a quick, awful thought that there might be embarrassing files or photos on my computer. But the feeling faded. The most risqué thing on my laptop was a picture of me in a bikini on vacation in Mexico, trying to get a spider monkey to hug me.

The sheriff's cell phone buzzed. He took it out of his pocket and checked his texts. He stood. "I've got to go."

"How's it going? The Germans talking?"

He sighed. "Their lawyer is a piece of work, to say the least. I'm not hopeful we'll be able to bring any charges against them. Besides, I'm not sure what laws they broke here."

"Any word on Tyler's condition?"

He held up his phone. "That's where I'm heading. He's stable and awake."

I got to my feet, despite my wobbly legs. I was likely still in shock. "I can go with you."

"Geez, Andi, let the man do his job," Ginny chastised. "You need to have a hot bath and some whisky and some sleep."

"Ginny's right. You need to take care of yourself."

"But—"

"I know what to ask the doc about the bloodwork," he said with a wry twist of his lips. He was humoring me, and I appreciated it. "I'm sure it will show exactly what you think it'll show. Thanks to your stubborn and tenacious nature, June will be out of jail and home in no time."

I smiled at him.

He smiled back.

Something passed between us, something significant. Not a kiss, but nearly as potent.

"I'll call you later." He dipped his head and went inside to talk to his deputies. After that, he left.

Ginny started, "Hey, sorry to have c—"

I put my hand up toward her. "Do not say what I think you're going to say, Ginny."

"I was going to say, 'Come between you two.'" She giggled. "What did you think I was going to say?"

I shook my head. "I've heard some of the language that comes out of your mouth."

"You should try it. It's liberating." She laughed and swung her arm around me. "Now, c'mon. Let's go to my place and drink lots of whisky and pass out. You deserve a good night's sleep."

I let her lead me back through my suite, out the door, then down the corridor to hers. I didn't have the heart to tell her that I didn't think I was going to sleep, whisky or not. There was too much going through my head. And none of it was good.

If someone was trying to scare me, he was doing one hell of a great job.

CHAPTER TWENTY-FIVE

GRAYING CLOUDS FLOATED BY the sun, blocking it out for a few minutes, as I walked down Main Street toward the marina. Mrs. Weiss was right. A rainstorm was brewing. I actually loved this kind of weather. It didn't rain much where I'd lived in California, so a rainstorm was a welcome event.

I lifted my face, enjoying the way the breeze came off the lake. It had a surprising salty tang to it, much like the ocean. Some days when I stood on the cliffs at the hotel and looked out over the vastness of the water, I imagined Lake Michigan was the Pacific.

I took in a deep breath of fresh, crisp air, and let it out slowly, relaxing my shoulders and neck. It had been a rough week, and I was still trying to brush off the negative remnants.

I'd moved into a new suite. It wasn't as large as the other one had been and didn't have the best view, but it would suffice until the new furniture arrived. The sofa, the mattress on the bed, the wardrobe, and the shelving unit in the living room all needed to be replaced. Everything else had been cleaned up, but the suite still felt dirty when I walked through it. I wasn't sure that feeling would go away. I'd considered asking Lois if I could just permanently move into another suite, but she'd done so much for me already, I didn't want to ask for more.

Twenty-four hours after the break-in, Sheriff Jackson had called to make sure I was okay and to let me know that I'd been right about Tyler and Brittany. They both had the same blood chemistry, the same amounts and content of poisons in their systems. It hadn't been one substance that had killed Brittany but a combination of them over a period of time. The same thing would've happened to Tyler eventually if the Germans hadn't been there to help him.

No one had murdered Brittany Gervais. She had inadvertently done it to herself. The coroner ruled it an accidental death. And because there was no murder, June had been released, all charges dropped.

It helped that Brittany's sister, Tracy, after some intense scrutiny from the sheriff, had recanted her claim that June had come to the mainland to see Brittany. And I had been right about Tracy's car being the one that June had damaged with the garden shears.

Corporate lawyers for Nature Path Pharmaceuticals and Ackerman Biosystems were set to descend onto the island to interview Tyler and the Germans, and to sort out the mess. I imagined, somewhere along the line, Tyler would be facing some serious consequences. Or maybe one of the companies would hire him, give him a lab, let him do what he and Brittany had planned to do, and they would all make some serious money.

After the sheriff had told me all that, he'd paused, and I could feel his nerves coming through the speaker on the phone. I'd paused, too, as I had no idea what to say to him. I knew what

I should've said: *I like you, Luke. Let's see where this goes,* but I was too chicken. And I hadn't actually broken up with Daniel, either. It wouldn't be right to put the moves on the sheriff while I was dating Daniel. Even Ginny would agree with that, even as she'd been needling me about the astonishingly gorgeous Clive Barrington.

After a super-long, uncomfortable pause, the sheriff had finally said, "Don't find any more bodies, Andi. I need a darn break."

I'd chuckled, but it wasn't heartfelt. I, too, needed a darn break. And that likely meant from everything. Including a stubborn, sexy sheriff who made my blood boil and my heart skip a few beats.

Finally, I'd said, "Me, too."

When I'd disconnected the call, I felt sad, and I didn't know why. For the next couple of days, that feeling stayed with me. Ginny thought I was getting depressed, so she tried at every turn to lift up my spirits and make me laugh. She'd been doing a good job. But after days of being cooped up in the hotel and under watchful eyes of the entire Park family, I made my escape and headed for a long walk through the village.

I didn't get far before I spied Clive Barrington strolling along Main Street, hands casually resting in the pockets of his khakis. The yellow golf shirt he wore accentuated his beautiful dark skin and made him seem sunny all over. He crossed the street to talk to me.

"Good evening, Ms. Steele. Lovely to see you," he said gallantly, in his even more lovely British accent. Why hadn't I noticed that accent the first time we'd met? Probably because I'd been too mesmerized by his sexy self.

I nodded. "Mr. Barrington. Are you coming from the Top of the Lilac?"

He smiled again, another megawatter. And those eyes. Ginny was right. Simply stunning. "Well, I was actually saving that one for a special occasion. Since it's your favorite, would you like to join me for dinner one evening?"

I didn't know exactly what to say to that, so I kept quiet.

"You did say that your job is to make sure I get whatever I want while I'm on Frontenac Island, did you not?" He arched his eyebrows and grinned. "I travel quite a bit, and I do tire of eating alone. I'd be honored if you'd join me for dinner tomorrow night." When I continued to pause, he said, "Please."

It was dinner. In a public place. Where I was well known. Surely there'd be no harm in it. But still, I felt a little nervous about it. I didn't normally dine with guests of the hotel. It was an invisible line I'd drawn for myself. Which meant I could cross it any time I wanted to.

I nodded. "Sure. I'd be happy to go. As I said, Top of the Lilac is my favorite place in town, outside of the Park."

"Excellent. Let's meet in the lobby at seven o'clock, and we can walk down together," he replied.

I nodded again. "I'll call for a reservation. And I'll see you then."

He tipped his head, and I had the silly impression that he'd have tipped his hat if he'd been wearing one. I watched him saunter away and wondered, *Just who are you, and what is it that you're up to, Mr. Clive Barrington from Hong Kong?*

I continued my walk and stopped in at June's Blooms, but the sign on the door said CLOSED. And I had a feeling that the sign wasn't going to change for some time.

After turning right into the marina—there was someone I wanted to see—I walked along the docks, taking in the different boats. Some were very large yachts. I'd heard there was a boat docked here worth more than two million dollars called the *Magpie*. Others were smaller skiffs made for sailing for a few hours on calm waters.

I turned to head down another dock, when I spotted a particular redhead standing at a vacant slip. As I approached, she turned toward me. I saw a pair of gardening shears in her hand, which reminded me of the time she'd used shears to damage a car. Why was she holding them now?

"Hey, June," I said cautiously.

"Hi, Andi."

Her hair was unruly, but her cheeks were flushed. She wore deck shoes and her usual blouse-and-ankle-pants outfit, as if she'd dressed for sailing. "What are you doing here?"

She turned and pointed the shears toward a boat docked there. I knew whose boat it was. She said, "I was just checking to see if he came back."

Simon Gervais had vanished after that night I'd seen him at the fountain. After I'd told the sheriff about Simon living on his boat in the marina, the sheriff had come down to check. The boat had been unoccupied and Simon was gone. The sheriff thought he'd taken a ferry to the mainland for a faster get away. He'd put out a BOLO, but we'd heard nothing more.

I looked at June. She seemed distant. Ungrounded. Barely holding herself together.

Simon's actions had broken June to pieces. She wasn't the same woman as before he'd betrayed her so cruelly. Before she had been accused of murder and gone to jail. That kind of trauma changes a person. She hadn't been capable of murder before, but Simon's actions might have pushed her too far.

"What are doing with the shears?" I asked carefully, with what I hoped was a playful lightness in my voice.

"What?" She seemed surprised, then she looked at the shears and shrugged. "I'd left them on the boat. Figured I'd take them back with me."

"Sure," I said. "That makes sense."

She looked and me, then down at the water. "He fell off the boat. Maybe hit his head or something. He was still here. All that time."

I followed her gaze. Which was when I saw Simon Gervais floating face up, his body lodged in the corner of the dock, banging against the sea wall. He'd been dead for days, from the look of him.

I peered more closely at June's shears. I didn't really believe June had used them to kill Simon. There was no fresh blood on them for one thing. And he really didn't look like a new kill. What did I know, though? He might have threatened her. She could have brandished the shears to fend him off. Maybe he'd stepped off the dock while he was coming after her. Whatever happened, the sheriff would sort things out. This time, I was going to stay out of it. I believed in June, and that's all that mattered. Poor woman.

I reached for my cell phone and called the sheriff. When he picked up, I told him where I was, who I was with, and what I'd seen.

"I'll be right there. Take June home and stay there with her until you hear from me," he said.

"Will do," I replied before I disconnected and dropped the phone into my pocket.

I patted June on the shoulder. "Do you want me to walk you home? We could grab a coffee along the way."

She nodded. Still dazed, she allowed me to remove the shears from her hand. I held them carefully to avoid contaminating any evidence the sheriff might find.

Together, we walked off the dock and onto the main street. As we passed various villagers, they smiled and said hello. Some of them gave June the side-eye, though. I hated to see it. Although she'd been cleared of all charges, there were still rumors floating around. That's what happened in a small town, I supposed.

We grabbed a coffee at Beano's and I asked for a bag. I slipped the shears into the bag and then we continued our walk.

"So, I was thinking of leaving," June said.

"For good?"

"I'm not sure. A few months, most likely." She closed her eyes and lifted her face to the sun. "I have some money saved up, and I'd like to travel. I haven't been anywhere. So I think it's time I go somewhere and see a few things."

"When would you go?"

"In a couple of weeks." She glanced at me, her eyes bright and clear. "I was thinking of starting in Italy. Have you ever been?"

I shook my head. "No, but I hear it's beautiful there."

She nodded, then was silent for a bit as we kept walking. Finally, we made it to her house and she turned to me. "Thank you for helping me."

"You're welcome, June."

She hugged me and then pulled back. "So, I was thinking of renting out my house for the months I'm gone." She gave me a small smile. "Do you know anyone who'd want to rent it?"

I returned her smile. "I might. Do you allow cats?"

"Absolutely."

ABOUT THE AUTHOR

Diane Capri is an award-winning *New York Times*, *USA Today*, and world-wide bestselling author. She writes several series, including the Park Hotel Mysteries, the Hunt for Justice, Hunt for Jack Reacher, and Heir Hunter series, and the Jess Kimball Thrillers. She's a recovering lawyer and snowbird who divides her time between Florida and Michigan. An active member of Mystery Writers of America, Author's Guild, International Thriller Writers, Alliance of Independent Authors, and Sisters in Crime, she loves to hear from readers and is hard at work on her next novel.

Please connect with her online:

http://www.DianeCapri.com

Twitter: http://twitter.com/@DianeCapri

Facebook: http://www.facebook.com/Diane.Capri1

http://www.facebook.com/DianeCapriBooks

Made in the USA
Coppell, TX
30 April 2020